THE PURSUIT

A MICHAEL VAUGHN NOVEL

Nick had sprinted far ahead, and he wasn't stopping. "Hey!" Vaughn yelled again, taking off after him. Leaving the rest of the group in the dust, he reached Nick's side. And as they pounded the ground side by side, he couldn't help himself: He reached out to give Nick's shoulder a shove.

They had run so far that they'd made it from the clearing where they usually finished out the runs into the sparsely wooded area a few hundred yards behind the dorm. "What do you want, golden boy?" Nick asked, giving Vaughn a manic grin and performing a sweep-kick so quickly that Vaughn found himself on his back before he even knew what was happening.

Vaughn got to his feet quickly, but not quickly enough. Nick had already reached the patio of the dorms. When Vaughn raced over to tackle him at the knees, they fell to the cracked concrete surface like two tons of bricks.

"WHAT THE HELL ARE YOU DOING?"

ALIAS™

THE PURSUIT

A MICHAEL VAUGHN NOVEL

LIZZIE SKURNICK

AN ORIGINAL PREQUEL NOVEL BASED ON THE HIT TV SERIES CREATED BY J. J. ABRAMS

BANTAM BOOKS
NEW YORK ✱ TORONTO ✱ LONDON ✱ SYDNEY ✱ AUCKLAND

Alias: The Pursuit

A Bantam Book / July 2003
Text and cover art copyright © 2003 by Touchstone Television

ISBN: 0-553-49402-3

Visit us on the Web! www.randomhouse.com

Published simultaneously in the United States and Canada

Bantam Books is an imprint of Random House Children's Books, a
division of Random House, Inc. BANTAM BOOKS and the rooster
colophon are registered trademarks of Random House, Inc.

PRINTED IN THE UNITED STATES OF AMERICA

OPM 10 9 8 7 6 5 4 3 2 1

THE PUCK SMASHED INTO the goal like a grenade exploding.

Making a quarter turn with his stick, Michael deftly flipped a new puck onto the ice from the quickly emptying bucket at his feet. Moving like a low-flying plane, he approached the goal and crossed the bar. Before another second had passed, an orange puck had smashed almost through the nubbly gray net and joined the other pucks scattered at the bottom of the goal.

At least I can still aim, Michael thought, looking with satisfaction at the growing constellation of pucks that had shot back onto the ice after being pounded inside the bounds. *Too bad I'm fifty thousand times too slow to be the next Wayne Gretzky.*

In the cold air of the rink, Michael's breath made plumes of smoke as he skated over to his bag to take a swig from his water bottle. *Though at this point, I'd be happy to take a job cleaning the ice.*

He surveyed the rows and rows of darkened seats that surrounded the rink. His loud, ragged breathing was the only sound in the place, that and the hum of the overhead fluorescents. Michael always snapped the lights on when he had these late-night practice sessions at Orca, an indoor ice rink with distinctive black-and-white patterning.

Michael took a long pull from his water bottle and placed the cap back on. A low, groaning sound suddenly seemed to rise from the benches around him, like a beast slowly waking. Michael tensed, snapping his head around to find the cause. Then his shoulders relaxed. The groan, he realized, had come directly from him.

Before Michael could stop it, another groan escaped, this one like the whoosh of air escaping a tire. He began to pound his chest as if he were having a choking fit. It seemed like the first real exhalation he had allowed himself in months, but for some reason, he was afraid. If he let himself feel anything right now, he might discover that he was filled with enough rage to smash up the whole arena.

Well, isn't that what hockey players are supposed to do? he thought, surprised to find a small smile making its way across his features, like a hiker clambering over unfamiliar terrain. *Maybe I'm cut out for a life on ice after all.*

A life on ice was right. Ever since he'd reached the spring of his senior year at Georgetown University, that's how he'd felt—shelved, on hold. Michael smiled again. This was easily his first real smile in months. Or at least his first real smile since he'd finally accepted the fact that no matter how hard he'd worked to fit the profile and prepare himself for his chosen career, no matter who his father was, the CIA just wasn't going to respond to the application he'd sent them nearly a year ago.

They hadn't even sent a form letter to acknowledge receipt.

Cursing and mumbling under his breath, Michael grabbed his bucket and skated back out onto the ice to begin the tedious task of rounding up all the pucks. Kneeling down to grasp one that had lodged under the skeleton of the goal, he slipped, then found himself sprawled out nearly full length under the battered hood, his ear smarting where he'd winged the side of the goal on his way down.

Michael looked up at the ceiling, the bulbs of the hanging orbs blinding him momentarily.

Now I'm really *on ice,* he thought. *And the CIA's sent my application to the penalty box.*

* * *

It had been a long, hot summer in D.C. A long senior year, in fact. And it would have been even longer without Nora.

Except now Nora was gone.

Michael had spent the fall like most Georgetown seniors: hanging out with friends, getting recommendations from all his best professors lined up, and of course, attempting to dutifully attend all the classes that suddenly seemed a little more voluntary now that it was all coming to an end. Luckily, Michael was a natural grind—finished with most of his coursework, he had picked up advanced classes in French, Italian, and Spanish, then blown by his classmates. Raised bilingual, with a French mother and an American father, Michael had always found Romance languages a breeze.

Until the first semester of his senior year, when he'd met Nora, Michael had felt only a vague impatience for college to end so that his career with the CIA could begin. But after he met Nora, it was almost as if he had split in two: There was the Michael who loved hanging out with his pretty, smart, sophisticated girlfriend, and there was the Michael who was planning to work for the American government the minute they got their act together and came for him.

Needless to say, the two Michaels had never even been introduced.

Michael met Nora in a beginner's art class, the one easy course he had allowed himself to take after three and a half straight years of hard-core international relations, with healthy doses of history and economics thrown in for good measure. Michael smiled again, thinking of his arrival that first day and his shock at the damp, cramped basement where the art class had met, so unlike the wood-paneled seminar rooms where he was used to debating whether to forgive the debt to Third World nations or what were the actual causes of World War I.

"You? Taking an *art* course?" his mother had chortled when Michael had informed her of his plan during one of his monthly calls to her northern

California retreat. He heard ice tinkling in a glass and knew she was probably out on her sun porch, holding a tall, frosted iced tea, watching the waves of the Pacific crash against worn-down pilings. She had moved to the rambling house when Michael had gone to college, and he loved to visit, taking breaks from his sucession of tiny dorm rooms, each with its own small leaded-glass window from which he watched the leaves change, fall, and grow back.

"They say some genetic traits take longer to express themselves than others," Michael had responded, laughing. Both he and his mother knew that although she had filled their house with enormous paintings and stylized, intricate sculptures in the years following his father's death—eventually even achieving a limited local fame for her own vivid, sun-splashed canvases—he had never graduated beyond the stick-figure montage most kids abandon after the first grade.

"Well, I've saved all your art so far," his mother said, sounding faintly bemused. Michael wondered if she was referring to the ancient crayon drawings of a dragon, a lizard, and some slug like object she had managed to coax from him at an early age and tape to the kitchen wall, before he learned he was happier playing with old radios and—once he got his first PC—computers. "I guess it won't kill me to tack up a few more masterpieces."

Michael had bought all the pads and charcoals the course required. Though the art supplies cost far more *dinero* than his used economics textbooks ever had, he was excited at the prospect of a course that didn't require his reading a packet as thick as a telephone book. As was his habit, he had arrived on time the first day, awkwardly wielding his sketch pad like a shield. An empty room stared back at him. There was only a scattering of stools, a bunch of tall metal easels tossed into a heap in the corner, and a large plywood platform in the center. Down the hall, Michael heard the rise and fall of approaching voices. He turned to see a group of students—could they possibly be freshmen?—all dressed in black, most of them with hair dyed colors Michael usually associated with nuclear fallout. A girl or boy—Michael couldn't tell—brushed by him on the way to the stack of easels. "Ex*cuse* me," he—she—*it* said, expertly hefting one of the steel skeletons to a standing position.

With every Andy Warhol clone that crossed the threshold holding a well-used portfolio like an old friend, Michael felt his spirits sinking. *They said this was a* beginner's *course,* Michael thought, wanting to be amused that he was getting panicky over an art course but horrified that his palms were actually sweating. *Why does everyone else seem like they would be at home in some Left Bank café?*

Watching the classroom fill, Michael noticed that *all* the newcomers—boys with piercings and chains, girls with black tights and platform shoes— seemed suspiciously handy with an easel. Michael felt particularly conspicuous as he tried to get his into a standing position. As a woman who looked like an older sister to the female students entered the room and mounted the platform, he found himself in a truly excruciating position, kneeling over the tangled legs of his easel like a farm boy trying to untip a cow.

"Please let me live," a voice whispered from above his right shoulder. Michael looked up, ready to let fly with some sarcasm of his own, but he stopped when he saw a brown-eyed, dark-haired beauty smiling down at him. She made a mock-strangulation move on her neck, as if to illustrate what he was doing to the poor pieces of metal. "I can't *stand* it!"

"You better *learn* to stand it . . . or stand *up*,"

Michael whispered back, finally sliding a bolt into the right catch so that the easel stood upright in what appeared to be a steady posture.

"See—you just had to give it some TLC," the girl whispered back, her eyes dancing. The woman on the platform was issuing directions. Michael looked around and saw that everyone one else—his new friend included—had clipped their pads to the easels and were holding large pieces of what looked like orange chalk at the ready.

Michael didn't even remember where he had left his pad. He was also pretty sure that he hadn't bought anything orange.

The girl assessed his situation and acted. "Quick," she whispered, passing him her piece of chalk and pulling one for herself from a plastic box filled with various artsy utensils. "Now find your pad, or Mireille will get mad."

Michael leaned closer. The girl smelled both delicious and dangerous—a light floral underlaid with something spicy. He knew he was in trouble. The few times he had fallen, it had always been for tall brunettes with dark, dark eyes. "Who's Mireille?" he hissed back.

A dark shadow approached his easel, like the cloud of an oncoming storm. Michael looked up into the pale blue eyes of a very angry woman. Mireille was the teacher, of course, and he was, he realized, probably very much in trouble.

"I am," she said in a—how could he have missed it?—commanding French accent. She could have come from the same Normandy region where his mother had been born.

"*Pardon, Madame,*" he replied automatically, as if he were speaking to his mother. Mireille's eyes flared as if he'd just cursed her out. She probably got a lot of mileage around these Americans for her accent, he realized. It must not be pleasant to find that one of her insolent students had the same one.

Michael switched back to English immediately. "I was just having a little trouble. . . ."

"*Making* trouble, you mean," Mireille interrupted. "And holding up my class. *Silence.* Class, this is Shannon," she said, gesturing to a redhead in a white robe who'd just emerged from the corner. As the class watched, Shannon mounted the platform, glared at all of them defiantly, and removed her robe.

Michael almost knocked over his easel.

The girl on the left leaned over to whisper to him again. Her eyes sparkled with mischief. "Don't worry," she said, shrugging and beginning to sketch. "We probably won't get around to you for a couple of weeks."

* * *

By the time fall turned decisively into winter—and by the time Nora explained that the art department actually *hired* nude models and didn't use the students in the class—he and Nora were almost inseparable. He moved most of his things into her attic apartment in a crumbling Victorian in Georgetown (her marigold walls and queen-sized futon were a big step up from his Spartan cell with its screeching cot), and they spent the semester seeing the blockbusters Nora adored two months late at the three-dollar theater, eating waffles and scrambled eggs at the corner diner, and drawing each other's feet and hands until both decided they weren't cut out for the art world and dropped Mireille's course.

Nora Carlisle was as unlike Michael as anyone he'd ever met. While he had majored in solid, unromantic disciplines, she has chosen (in his opinion) the goofiest, most made-up major in the world next to sociology: psychology. Time after time, he argued that she was wasting her brains on a bunch of nonsense created by "spiritual" Europeans. "Believe me, Freud didn't know anything," he argued. "Why don't you become a mathematician instead?" He knew that her clinical work involved some complex equations even her advisor couldn't follow. "Or become a real doctor, for heaven's sake?"

Nora was always unruffled by his pleas. "Your insistence that your personality isn't worth studying" she would say, planting a gentle kiss on his head, "is exactly what makes studying you so interesting to me."

And the differences only multiplied. While Nora had gone to a huge, urban public school, where daughters of diplomats and sons of janitors took SAT prep side by side, Michael had attended the same small, private boys' school his father had gone to, mixing with the sons of his father's old friends. While Nora knew everyone, everywhere—the lady behind the counter in the deli, a group of freshman girls trying to sell raffle tickets at the train station, the dean of the Environmental Sciences department—Michael had only a few close friends. And most important, while Nora had an enormous family back in New York—so large that she claimed she couldn't take the subway without running into a cousin or uncle—Michael had only his mother; his father had died in the line of duty. (According to his mother, there was an extremely distant and extremely religious set of cousins still in France somewhere, but she claimed she'd pretend to be someone else if they tried to contact her.)

Sometimes that year, Michael was almost sure that what he was feeling was what everybody else called *love*. Did he *love* seeing Nora every day? Check. Did he *love* arguing with her so fiercely over a movie that he didn't even notice until the last minute that she was sneaking the last piece of bacon from his plate? Check. Did he *love* the way his stomach flipped at the sight of her approaching in her trademark fringed jacket and worn cowboy boots? Definite check.

But did he love *her*?

Rain check.

He loved their time together—watching her hushed concentration over her psychology books, seeing how efficiently she managed the lab where she'd worked all four years of school, hearing the shout of her laughter during funny parts in movies—sometimes so loud that people shushed them—so it seemed probable that he was *in* love. But it was a funny kind of love, he was sure. His feelings for Nora were like jewels kept behind glass, guarded by an intricate burglary system.

Michael could look at what was under the glass, but he couldn't touch what was inside.

With a sigh, Michael skated slowly across the ice, considering. The CIA had been the big unspoken issue between him and Nora all along. *The CIA and my father*. He picked up a puck and threw it, sending it skittering.

Michael didn't hide his father's death from his close friends at school—they knew he had died when Michael was eight. But most of his friends were male, and men weren't big on poking around at obviously painful places or wanting to talk about their feelings.

Though, for all Michael's fears about telling Nora about his father's death, neither was she. When, a month into their relationship, he had given her the brief run-through of his family history, Nora was silent. "You're doing that psychology thing, aren't you?" Michael finally asked. "Not saying anything so I'll tell you about the bodies in the basement?"

Nora simply continued to look at him and held up the wooden spoon from the soup she was stirring. "Is that what *you* think I'm doing?" she asked lightly.

Michael let out a very audible groan. "If you're

going to play doctor——" he began, but Nora held up a warning spoon for him to stop.

"I'm sorry," she broke in. "I didn't mean to be flip. I just figure that if you ever want to *really* talk about it, you'll tell me."

Michael expected to feel relief at her words but instead felt as if steel bands were tightening around his chest. *Am I mad that she doesn't want to know more?* he asked himself, watching her calmly stir the split-pea soup that had been simmering all day. *Or am I just scared of telling her more?* The bands started to become a straightjacket.

Nora looked at him, and this time, something in her gaze immediately dissolved all his anxiety. "Sweetie, please don't worry," she said, holding her free hand out toward him. He took it. "The soup isn't going to be so bad this time, I promise." They both laughed, and suddenly it was over.

And that had been the first and only time they'd ever talked about his father. Michael didn't even know what he would have been able to add to the story. He didn't know much, except that his father had worked for the CIA and that he'd been killed in the line of duty. After his father's death, he and his mother had returned briefly to France, then moved to California. Until he went away to high school, the two had made the pilgrimage once a year to his father's grave, eaten dinner at a restaurant that had always looked to Michael like the inside of a funeral home—stiff white cloths and heaps of flowers—then returned to California, where his mother took him to soccer and hockey practices as usual and cheered on the sidelines at his games. There was an album filled with photographs of them as a family on a shelf in the living room, but he hadn't taken it down since he was ten.

Don't forget about the plans, Michael thought, coming to a stop. He rubbed the tough part of his glove along the side of his skate blade, an old nervous habit. *How you never told Nora what you were* really *planning to do after college.*

Like everyone else that senior year, Michael was consumed with fear and excitement about what was ahead. But he had also had a secret: While he had applied for advanced degree programs in economics and international studies at all the best universities and been accepted to most of them, he wasn't planning on going to school. He'd had known what he wanted to do ever since he'd watched four men lower his father's coffin unsteadily into the ground and his mother's hand had clamped down like a vise on his left shoulder.

Follow his father into the CIA.

While Michael hadn't known much about what his father had done when he was very young, over the years he had gleaned enough information to put the pieces together.

He remembered the cold night in November—the fifth anniversary of his father's death—when his mother had finally told him what his father had done for a living, explaining that he hadn't worked for the state department. "He worked for the CIA, Michael," she'd said, her voice breaking. "And while I was never able to know exactly what he was working on when he died, I know that he gave his life in service to his country." Her hand had covered his and her accent had deepened. "Michael, I always want you to know that I loved your father very much, and it was very hard to lose him. But still"—and here she gave way entirely to tears—"I cannot help being very proud of him."

Michael didn't cry—he hadn't cried since his father's funeral. "Mom, I'm not stupid," he said, squeezing her hand in support. "I figured out what Dad did a long time ago. It's what I want to do, too."

It had been another night in November when he

had headed out to the computer lab to finally do what he'd thought about a million times: fill out the online application for the CIA. He felt a surge of something as he finally pressed the Send button. Excitement? Fear? Exhilaration?

It was *living*.

And while Michael knew that he wanted to feel that way when he was with Nora, too, somehow their time together wasn't even close to being that *real*.

So in August, after a summer of driving to the shore to visit friends on weekends and dropping Nora off at the lab before he headed to his job as a research assistant for one of his old economics professors, Nora and Michael finally parted in front of their apartment before she drove up to New York to begin her program in clinical psychology at Columbia.

"Michael, let me write you first, okay?" Nora asked, her eyes shining with tears. For moving day, she was wearing old Converse high-tops and cut-offs, and he thought she had never looked more beautiful.

"Okay," he said, gently stroking the side of her face.

They'd argued it over and over. Nora had practically begged Michael to go to one of the programs that had accepted him on the East Coast, so that they could at least stay in close touch, if not together. "You're breaking up with me," Nora had said. "You don't realize you are, but that's what you're doing."

"Nora, it doesn't have anything to do with you," Michael had said. "I just have to get away from here."

What he couldn't tell Nora was that he was miserable and he had to get away. Because as remarkable as it was, the CIA hadn't called. And like a rejected suitor, part of him felt that if he couldn't be a part of the CIA, he had to get away from the United States entirely for a while.

But leaving Nora was harder in person than in theory. "Just please don't come home with one of those stupid Swiss girls," Nora joked, smiling through her tears. Michael felt a lump in his throat and pulled her close to him.

If he could only tell her the truth—that just the word *Swiss* made him feel sick. Every stupid program he had applied to had offered him the works: a free ride; minimal teaching duties; housing stipends. He'd chosen the University of Geneva. As much as he'd loved his work in college, he had never dreaded anything so much in his life. *Once I have a Ph.D. in economics*, he thought, *the CIA better give me a second look.*

"I'm not really into Swiss economists," Michael said, trying to smile. *Or Swiss anything,* he wanted to add.

Nora gave him a gentle punch in the arm. "It's not really the economists I'm worried about," she said.

The weeks since she'd gone had been dry and dusty as old books: an endless succession of papers for his boss, unmemorable pool halls, and late-night hockey sessions at Orca. Now it was his turn. His bags were packed, and tomorrow he would board a train for New York, where he would catch the plane that would finally take him to Geneva.

Could I have really told Nora about my plans? Michael asked himself. *Maybe not being able to talk about my plans—and about my past—was a big part of why I never felt really close to her.*

You think? Michael could almost hear her re-plying, with her trademark sarcasm. Although he often made fun of Nora's chosen profession, he knew that the accuracy of her insights often made him blush. *You don't need to be Sigmund Freud to figure this one out.*

Finally Michael chose not to examine Nora's insights and just focus on the present. He was going to the University of Geneva, that was all—and then let the CIA try to keep him out.

"Ready, aim, fire," he said now with more heartiness than he really felt. He held up the last puck and with all his strength hurled it across the frigid expanse.

"Not bad," a voice called from the darkness.

2

WHEN THE VOICE CALLED out to Michael from the stands that summer night, he wasn't surprised—he assumed it was one of his old pool buddies or a study friend stopping by to take him out for a celebratory beer. In fact, his spirits lifted at the prospect. "Who's there?" he yelled back happily, speed-skating across the rink. Snapping guards on his blades, he stuck his gear into his bag and threw it over his shoulder.

But the man who emerged from the upper stands was no one Michael knew. Middle-aged, average height, carrying a gray trench coat over his left arm, he looked like anyone's ordinary business-man father—except for his eyes. As he and Michael approached each other, the man's eyes, black and bottomless, locked onto Michael and drew him deeper, like an undertow. "Michael Vaughn," he said. It wasn't a question.

"Yes," Michael heard himself say, and held his hand out. The other man took it and gripped it lightly, but for a second he seemed to Michael like a space traveler returned years later, one for whom shaking hands was a custom he had long since forgotten.

"My name's Les Ryan. I understand you're leaving town tomorrow."

Michael nodded. For a second he had the absurd thought that the man was some official from Georgetown come to collect a huge library fee or rescind a course credit before Michael skipped the country. *You think you can just drop an art course with one of our most esteemed professors and waltz on out of here, huh?*

Michael shook off the thought. The university did withhold diplomas for library fees or other unpaid charges, of course, but he had received his in May with the rest of his classmates. And like the rest of his buddies, he had immedi-ately handed the rolled document over to his mother, who had framed it and hung it over the mantel.

"Mr. Vaughn?" the man asked again. "Is that the case?"

"I'm sorry," Michael said, trying to focus. "It's just that I'm trying to figure out who you are."

The man didn't crack a reassuring smile or in any way try to make the usual pleasantries. "I'm a government official. I'm here to discuss certain things related to your application."

"I'm sorry, but I'm not sure what application you're referring to," Michael said. He was suddenly filled with irritation. Could the University of Geneva be having a problem processing his student visa?

Les Ryan looked closely at Michael, and Michael stared back. Suddenly, his visitor seemed to remember how human beings cracked a smile.

"That's not bad, Mr. Vaughn," Les Ryan said. "Let's go and get ourselves a cup of coffee, shall we?"

* * *

Considering the CIA's association with spies, espionage, and international warfare, Michael felt that the commencement of his career was oddly dull. It started with a cup of extremely subpar coffee at the old greasy spoon that had been a favorite of Nora's.

Over two cups of brown sludge, Les explained that it might be months before Michael even reached the career trainee—CT—stage at the CIA. That is, if he reached it at all. "Clearance and security checks can take awhile."

"How much of a while?" Michael prodded. He was only too happy to dispense with the University of Geneva for the time being, but it wasn't clear what he was supposed to do with himself while the CIA sent out officers to interview everyone who'd ever known him—though when he thought about it, it was not a particularly long list.

Les drained his cup. "Could be two months," he offered, his forehead crinkling as he looked off into space. "Then again, could be two years."

Michael blanched. "What am I supposed to do in all that time?"

Les raised his shoulders and then let them fall. "You can do whatever you want," he said, "as long as you remember that what goes on between us stays between us. As I said, though, it could be awhile, so you might want to keep your day job." He raised his cup and tapped it. "Waitress!"

Michael tried to keep Les's attention. "But my day job was going to be attending the University of Geneva," he said pointedly.

Michael's tone worked—it got the man's attention. Les gave him a sharp look, as if taking his measure, and then his face returned to his blank, genial neutrality—the Switzerland of faces. "Like I said, do what you want," Les said, slurping at the refill the waitress had just provided. "But it's going to be hard for us to continue the interview process if you go to Switzerland."

Michael tried to relax. He wanted to explain to Les that he wasn't trying to be difficult, he'd just always hated uncertainty. The period Les seemed to be talking about was a long time to wait for an answer that might not come—or to hang around doing nothing.

Michael had doctored his coffee with four creamers and a half-dozen sugar packets to make it vaguely palatable. He pushed at the muddy brew with a stirrer, breaking the film that had formed on the surface. Sure, he could probably continue with his job as a research assistant for his old professor, get a new crappy apartment. But wouldn't it get back to Nora somehow that he was still at school? And wouldn't she wonder why?

"Why don't you consider figuring out a good

cover your first assignment," Les said, possibly hiding another smile with a sip of his coffee.

Michael cracked his knuckles—he was talking to the CIA, after all, not some dopey human resources assistant. *I don't think they'd bother wasting their manpower on giving me the runaround,* he thought, almost smiling at the thought of being strung along by the CIA. He'd seen his friends agonize for months over summer jobs with various labs and law firms, waiting in vain for a reply to the endless white envelopes they sent out. *Well, here's the reply to my little white envelope,* he thought. *I'm sure once the CIA is at the one-on-one stage, they're pretty efficient at telling you no.*

Or yes.

"I guess for a while I can still be . . . going to the University of Geneva," Michael hazarded.

Les nodded. "Sounds good. And you never know; sometimes these clearance checks can go pretty fast."

Lucky I left things the way I did with Nora, Michael mused, realizing that, in the current hazy guidelines of their quasi-relationship, it wouldn't be weird for him not to write for quite a while— maybe even a few months. His mother wouldn't worry either—a quick email or note to let her know he'd arrived and she'd be taken care of. She'd told him she'd long ago given up trying to get him on the phone in person more than once or twice a month, and she certainly wouldn't expect even that frequency when he was overseas.

With few close friends, no inquisitive parents or siblings, and no girlfriend at home to lie to, Michael was suddenly and painfully aware that he must fit what the CIA was sure to call their perfect psychological profile. In fact, he'd surpassed it: At this point, he didn't even really have a home. His stuff was packed up, and he'd left his forwarding address with the super.

I'm more ready for the CIA than I thought, Michael realized.

The thought wasn't entirely comforting.

* * *

The next couple of steps didn't get any more glamorous. As he rented a car and temporarily took a room in a dreary residential hotel about an hour from Georgetown, Michael inwardly groused that this was certainly an odd way to begin a career involving spies and international intrigue.

Let's hope we get to the spy part soon, he thought.

But they didn't. Over the next few weeks,

Michael had several scheduled "dates" with Les, during which, over coffee, Les would grill Michael on every aspect of his life since he'd been born, from his favorite nursery school activities to his thesis in economics—of which, of course, Les already had a copy.

At these meetings, Les gave away almost nothing about himself or what he already knew about Michael, except to let Michael know that he hadn't needed to apply to the CIA after all—the CIA had been keeping an eye on him and his academics throughout his college career, tipped off by an economics professor who worked for them in a recruitment capacity.

"We were happy enough to learn of your enthusiasm for the prospect of joining us, though," Les said, leaning down to hide one of his rare smiles.

Michael flushed at the thought of the admittedly gung-ho answers he'd given to all the "Why do you want to join the CIA?" questions. "And you're not going to let me know who that professor is, I'm thinking," Michael said, reaching for the check. Although Les never allowed him to pay it, it had become their little routine.

"No," Les said shortly. However diligently Michael prodded him, Les remained a no-nonsense kind of guy.

After a few more interviews, Les invited him to a larger recruitment event. It had been nearly a month since Michael had supposedly gone to Geneva, and he'd spent the greater part of that time at a local motel, catching up on his reading. He was almost at the end of his tether, going stir-crazy from having nowhere to go and nothing to do, when he realized something that made his boredom seem a little more bearable.

Although it was true that CIA careers were billed as being glamour and action 24/7, his work with the CIA would likely involve a lot of exactly this kind of waiting. Slowly accumulating and analyzing bits of information, he would always be waiting for a break so he could move on something or someone. "Just pretend it's your first assignment," Les had said. All right, that's what he would do. For all he knew, the CIA jumped on people during career transitions specifically to see how they stood up under pressure—or lack of it.

As he got dressed to go, Michael was hoping that Les's invitation to this event meant he'd made it to another level—and thus was one step closer to getting out of his motel room. The address Les had given him was a Holiday Inn about two hours away, a beige monolith off an artery of the interstate. Wearing a suit and tie for the first time in months, Michael walked into a conference room teeming with other recruits, perhaps three or four hundred in all.

Michael didn't know whether he'd expected three people or three thousand, but somehow he was taken aback by the crush of people. *How many other people put their lives on hold for this chance?* he wondered, a competitive streak flaring up. *Or does everyone else just meet with the CIA on his or her lunch break?*

"Jeez, this could be any graduate student conference," a pretty Asian woman next to Michael commented. They were hanging back from the main part of the crowd: a huge group clustered around the banquet tables who were loading up on canapés. Some other scattered recruits seemed to be staying on the sidelines, as if they were afraid of their hosts, who, lurking in the corner like vultures, were all wearing Les's no-nonsense mask, battered gray suit, and credentials on their clip-on IDs.

Michael had checked around for Les, but he hadn't seen him amongst the gray ghosts. Now he looked more closely at the animated crowd of twenty- and thirty-somethings. Everyone was dressed in business standard: the women with minimal makeup and sensible shoes, the men with crisp shirts and red power ties. He himself, after a fierce internal debate, had chosen a more decorous blue.

Michael grinned down at the woman. "You mean it's *not* a graduate student conference?" he asked, downing his ginger ale in one swallow. "My advisor's gonna have to answer for this."

That day, alongside the other hopefuls, Michael sat through what seemed like an endless battery of psychological, analytical, and physical tests, including a lie detector test. He signed about a million nondisclosure agreements. He gave the officers the number at the hotel where he was staying, and finally, about ten hours later, he was discharged.

In the hotel lobby he ran into the Asian woman he'd met earlier. She looked as fatigued as he felt, a gray tinge marring the oyster white of her skin.

Despite her obvious weariness, she seemed glad to see him. "Some day, huh?" she offered brightly.

He was glad for her friendly smile, and glad to speak to someone who didn't seem to want to fire questions at him or take his pulse twice every hour while he used a Stairmaster. "Unbelievable," he agreed. He knew by now it was strictly verboten to talk to outsiders about the experience they'd just had, but they were allowed to talk to each other, weren't they? And this woman didn't seem like one of the brown-nosers who were already adopting the grim-faced silence of their interrogators in imitation.

"Want to get a cup of coffee?" he asked. "We could compare notes."

She gave him a guarded look, as if he were yet another test, then jingled her car keys back at him. "Gotta get home to the wife and kids," she laughed, then made a face and sighed. "I'm just kidding, you know. My husband absolutely hates it when I call him that. It's just that this is such an old-boy organization. It gets my back up."

They began to move toward the hotel exit. Michael held the lobby door open for her as she sailed through into the parking lot, still talking. "And some people think that part of the reason the CIA doesn't release employee statistics is so that it doesn't have to obey federal guidelines regarding the hiring of women and minorities."

"Which way's your car?" Michael asked, trying not to sound as if he were interrupting. They hadn't made much progress into the parking lot yet, and though he found what she was saying intriguing, he wasn't sure he wanted to talk about the politics of the CIA right in front of the doors out of which all the G-men might come flying any minute. "I'm Michael Vaughn, by the way," he said, sticking out his hand for her to shake.

She had an incredibly strong grip. "I'm Akiko Schwartz," she replied, pumping up and down so firmly Michael could barely hide his wince. "Are you offering to walk me to my car? That's very thoughtful."

"I was trying to be," Michael said, rubbing his just-released hand with relief as they set off in the direction she had pointed. He couldn't believe how much pain his right hand was in. "But Akiko, seriously—if anyone bothers you, just offer to shake his hand."

Akiko turned back and saw Michael still rubbing his knuckles, then let out a loud burst of laughter. "I'm sorry," she said, although to Michael she sounded more merry than apologetic. "It's the new reps I'm doing. My husband says I'm getting the arms of a steamfitter."

Michael didn't know what a steamfitter's arms looked like, but he figured they must *feel* like bunched balls of iron to crunch his hand like Akiko just had. "You got that strong just from weight training?" he asked. They'd reached her car, a small red hatchback, and she waited a moment before inserting her keys in the door.

"Well, I'm a black belt in Aikido, too," she said, shrugging as if it were nothing. "And I like to do a little Ultimate Fighting on the side."

Michael had seen Ultimate Fighting matches on TV, where boxers and Greco-Roman wrestlers were smacked off their feet by wiry men using jujitsu or tae kwon do. He'd never seen a woman fight in one of those matches, but he was willing to bet that Akiko could kick some serious butt. "That might have something to do with it," Michael commented dryly.

Akiko got into her car and rolled down the driver's-side window. "Good luck, Michael," she said, suddenly looking serious. "You seem like a nice guy—I think you'd be good to work with."

Michael was struck by her directness, and also pleased by it. There was no explanation for it, but he found that he was feeling the same way, and strongly—as if they'd known each other for years instead of minutes. Maybe it was like the bonding old veterans said wartime foxholes produced.

"Good luck to you, too," he said. "And all my best to the wife."

Akiko grinned and started the engine. She stuck her head out her window for one last comment. "If I don't make it, they're going to have a big problem," she said, smiling widely. "In my day job, I'm a civil rights lawyer with the justice department."

Michael laughed with her and waved his non-sore hand as she gunned the motor and drove off. He set off toward his own car, his energy somehow restored by the brief encounter. He thought about Akiko's firm manner, her interesting factoids, and her killer grip.

If every recruit's that impressive, he mused, *I might have a harder time making it into the CIA than I thought.*

3

THREE WEEKS LATER, LES called and gave
Michael another date and time to show up at the hotel. "They're not going to make me hold my breath
underwater again, are they?" Michael asked. The
test during which he and ten other recruits had been
forced to descend to the bottom of the pool holding
bricks bars and bring them up and down as many
times as they could in two minutes had been one of
the more unpleasant of his experience.

"The whole interview's underwater, kid," Les
said gruffly, then signed off. *Something must be
happening with my application,* Michael thought as

he put down the receiver, *because Les is definitely loosening up. Let's just hope it isn't that they're about to drop me and he doesn't care what he says.*

This time Michael found himself alone in the lobby, and he was called into a private room, not a teeming conference room. Five people he'd never seen sat in leather executive chairs behind a large glossy table, and he sat in front of them on a simple four-legged steel seat, without even a side table on which to place a glass of water.

They introduced themselves as CIA officers, and their questioning began simply. "Do you feel that you have any impediments to serving the American government honestly and truthfully?" asked a man with a salt-and-pepper brush cut and a habit of spinning his pencil between his thumb and forefinger.

Instead of giving them the stock answer he'd used in all the previous sessions, Michael found something different flying out of his mouth before he could stop them. "Are you asking that because of my father?" he asked.

Michael was momentarily terrified at what he'd said, then glad. *After all, my father did work for them until he died,* he thought. *It seems silly not to bring it up.*

The man sitting at the center of the table flipped his pencil over and stopped. He looked to the woman on his left. She was solid and tall, in her fifties, with long, graying brown hair, and looked like an aging folk singer. She cocked her head to the right, a move so slight Vaughn almost missed it. *Nora always told me that's a typical sign your opponent is getting his dander up,* he thought, remembering her lectures to him on body language.

"Do *you* think that's why we're asking you?" she shot back.

Michael had to stop himself from laughing out loud. He thought again of Nora holding the soup spoon and giving him the psychologist's stock response to all questions. Clearly, this lady was willing to volley questions with him until he ducked for cover.

It was time to come out with his guns blazing.

"What can you tell me about my father's service?" he asked, looking at each of the five assembled officers in turn. It was the first pointed question he'd asked during the entire recruitment process, but it was starting to seem that he might benefit from a little dose of Akiko Schwartz's directness.

None of the officers looked away, but the

female officer's face closed like a door. "That's classified," she snapped.

Michael was afraid he'd blown it, but a few days later, he got another call from Les. It was the call he'd been waiting for all year, and Les had to repeat himself five times before he believed it. Les was calling to give him his EOD—Enter on Duty— the date on which he was to report at CIA headquarters: Langley.

"Congratulations," Les said once he'd finally managed to convince Michael he was telling the truth. "They said you held your breath pretty well," he joked.

Michael hung up the phone, the words echoing. *Held your breath.* That was exactly what he had been doing for almost a year, and now he didn't have to anymore.

Michael looked around at the dingy brownand-beige hotel room that had been his temporary home during his interrogation period. A long rip cut through the pilled and yellowing curtains, and a leak had caved in the portion of the ceiling over the bed almost to the breaking point.

He felt a surge of joy. He hadn't noticed how crummy the room was before this moment. Maybe he'd been scared to look at it too closely before he'd known for sure that he'd be leaving it soon.

Let's hope my powers of observation seem a little bit better to the folks in Washington, he thought, a wide grin cracking his face. He picked up the phone and set it on his lap, clenching the receiver between his ear and shoulder. His fingers hovered over the grid of buttons.

Who was he going to call first?

Slowly he felt the grin leave his face, and he returned the receiver to the cradle and the phone to the end table. *I can't tell Mom,* he thought, something closer to misery edging out the happiness of a moment before. *And I can't tell Nora.* He looked up at the water stain above him, the bowed ceiling suddenly seeming prophetic. *The only people in the world I can tell what just happened to me are the ones who already know.*

Michael leaned back on the bed, smacking his head on the headboard for good measure. It seemed like someone driving the point home for emphasis.

This is the way it's going to be from now on, that person would say. He'd be in a gray suit, strictly no-nonsense, and he'd dole out his smiles like a miser with a pocket full of pennies.

So get used to it.

*   *   *

Michael's EOD was the day after the next: Once the CIA made a decision, it seemed, they didn't waste any time. After he'd settled his plane tickets to Dulles, Michael swung by the strip-mall post office where he'd been forwarding all his mail. He hadn't bothered to check the box since he'd gotten it, sure it was crowded only with credit-card offers. Still, there was a chance that there could be something important in there as well.

Like a letter from Nora, possibly.

She'd be writing you in Geneva, dude, Michael told himself, pulling neatly into a parking spot. *Not to your old college address. Get a grip.*

But what if Nora *had* tried to write him in Geneva? he wondered suddenly. He hadn't made any arrangements for his mail to be forwarded from there. If she had written him care of the university, then received a "No such person exists at this address" message from the incredibly efficient Swiss mail, what would she be thinking now?

Stop driving yourself crazy, he cautioned himself. *First of all, Nora wouldn't write you in another country until she'd gotten your correct address. Second, if she called the university and couldn't find you, she'd just figure that they had screwed up.*

Still, the upsurge he'd felt after leaving his depressing beige cell had positively soured. He was feeling almost nauseated by the time the man behind the counter emerged with what looked like a year's worth of catalogs, plus a bulky brown package.

Michael handed over the new change-of-address form for Langley he'd just filled out and took the package, flipping it over. In her typically ornate script, his mother had addressed it to him care of the economics department at the University of Geneva.

Michael let out a low whistle. It was exactly the scenario he'd just been worrying about.

Michael began to retrace all the steps he'd taken to tie up his loose ends before leaving town. He'd informed the school that he was taking another semester to think over his options, and they'd agreed to hold his position for half a year. *The department must have just sent it to my old address,* Michael realized with relief. *And it got forwarded here.*

But when he turned the package over for the telltale yellow forwarding strip, there was nothing but smooth brown paper.

In fact, the package was oddly free of marks. Usually when something got sent back from abroad, it was practically covered in *PAR AVION*s and other stamps. But this only seemed to have the stamp of the local post office.

Is the CIA monitoring my mail? Michael wondered. The thought was a little scary. If they were, he hoped that didn't include reading it. He didn't care if they flipped through a J. Crew catalog, but it was against the law for them to read his letters, wasn't it?

Maybe the law was different for CIA recruits

"When did this come in?" Michael asked the man behind the counter, holding up the package.

The man shrugged. Michael had become so used to providing specific dates and circumstances, he'd temporarily forgotten how the real world ran. Clearly, they were a little more laissez-faire about such things as dates and times at Stamps "R" Us.

The man had roused himself, though, and was flipping through some pages on a clipboard. He looked up, surprised. "There's no record of a package at all," he said slowly. For a moment, it seemed like he was going to take the package back. "It's not for you?" he asked.

"It's for me," Michael answered, feeling more and more panicked by the minute. If the CIA was already monitoring and controlling his mail, did that mean they were listening in on the phone, too?

What if he *had* called Nora, or his mother, and told them what was happening? Would their offer have been revoked?

But maybe he was just being paranoid. "You don't keep any other records?" Michael asked hopefully. All this prying and poking could make anyone see conspiracies in coincidences. Maybe he had filled out a forwarding order for the Geneva address and just forgotten. Maybe all the stamps had fallen off. Or maybe this was all the result of the post office's Byzantine record-keeping policies.

The man shrugged. His previous languor crept back across his features like wine spilled onto thirsty fabric. He was content, it seemed, to chalk up the omission to the realm of eternal mystery.

"Forget it," Michael said, and left.

Back at his hotel room, Michael turned the parcel over and over. Finally he convinced himself that he was just being silly. *You filled out that card for Geneva, too,* he told himself. *And you're acting like your mother never writes you, when she sends you at least two or three letters every year.*

Just not usually packages, he thought, trying to force the thought back down even as it asserted itself more vigorously. He didn't know what he was scared of. Certainly the CIA would have no reason to send him anything weird or dangerous in the mail—and they wouldn't need to pretend to be his mother to get him to open it, either.

That thread of logic finally convinced him that he had nothing to worry about. He steeled himself and ripped the paper straight from end to end. A notebook held together by a rubber band with some kind of note clipped to the front spilled out onto his lap.

He breathed a sigh of relief. *Idiot.*

He slid the note out from under the rubber band and unfolded it. It was his mother's writing, but it was uncharacteristically brief. In fact, it wasn't even addressed to him. His mother also had left off her typically flowery signature. At first glance, it was just three lines on an otherwise empty page.

Some men came to see me about your security clearance. You must be working on some interesting things in Geneva, yes? And the Swiss are as thorough as they've always been.

The fourth line was so faint he almost missed it. It was in a spidery, crawling hand that looked like it had been almost erased or rubbed out—but not quite.

I thought you might be interested in this

Michael turned the contents of the package over in his hand. It was an ordinary ruled notebook, somewhat worse for the wear, small enough to almost fit in a jacket pocket. The spiral had come apart from the top half of the pages, but someone had recently made an effort to keep them together. The rubber band was clearly new.

He gently pulled the rubber band off and let the notebook fall open. Unsure what to think, he stared at the contents. Each line crawled with a series of numbers in an unfamiliar hand. They were written with a black ballpoint pen, by someone who had pressed heavily enough to make an impression on the pages on both sides. There were no discernable spaces between the numbers, but it seemed probable—even to Michael's untrained eyes—that they were some kind of code.

Michael flipped back a few pages, then looked quickly and carefully through the whole notebook. The pen sometimes changed from black ink to blue, but otherwise the blocks of numbers marched steadily toward some unknown destination.

What in the world was this notebook, and why had his mother sent it to him?

Michael's first instinct was to just call his mother and ask her. Something stopped him, however—the same thing that had given him pause at the post office.

If the CIA knew about the notebook, maybe he

wasn't supposed to talk about it. In fact, maybe it was some kind of test.

And if they don't know about it, Michael thought, *I'm not really sure I want them to.*

The last thought came out of nowhere, and Michael couldn't say what filled him with such certainty. He just had a strong hunch that whatever it was, he should keep it to himself for a while.

And if they ever ask about it, he thought, *I'll know it's some kind of test.*

Michael hated the trips and turns his mind was suddenly taking. He felt as if he were in some cheesy spy flick instead of getting ready to join one of the most effective and honorable government institutions in America—one that had taken on an even deeper significance in recent years. *Stop getting all Tom Clancy,* he badgered himself. *Government work is serious, and it's purely analytical. It has nothing to do with stupid feelings that come up out of nowhere.*

By sticking the notebook into the bottom of his backpack and finding the silliest comedy on TV he could locate, he managed to settle his feelings of disquiet. The next morning, only the faintest ghost of his thoughts the night before remained.

You were just being stupid, he told himself on

the way to the airport. *I bet it even has a name, like pre-CIA jitters. The same as medical students who think they're getting every illness they study. But in the case of CIA recruits, you start seeing conspiracies in all the ordinary things going on in your own life.*

By the time he returned the car to the rental agency, he'd regained most of his excitement. *You're going off to the CIA! Everything you worked for is finally happening! And instead of being ecstatic, you're worrying that someone is tapping your phone or sending you notebooks under your mom's name.*

It wasn't until he was up in the air somewhere over New York that he was finally able to put his finger on what had been bothering him.

While it was true that the note wasn't that different from his mother's usual letters, it differed from them in one major respect, something far more obvious than its lack of a proper greeting or sign-off. It was so obvious that he'd missed it completely.

His mother had grown up in France, and while she could converse perfectly well in English, with Michael—*avec Michel*—she always spoke in her native tongue: on the phone, in person—really any time except when they were joined by someone who only spoke English.

The notes she'd written him over the years were all in French.

But this note was in English.

"SHOOTERS ON THE LINE," a voice barked. The area fell silent. "Eyes and ears." There was a rustle as twenty hands adjusted goggles and headphones, then virtual silence after everyone had assumed the proper stance. The speaker dragged out the heavy quiet for a few seconds, letting it settle over the waiting bodies. Finally, there was a decisive bark:

"On my command!"

Michael tried to steel himself from taking a step backward. He knew many of his fellow trainees were doing likewise. That had been their first mistake as a group—instinctively cringing in anticipation of the loud reports of ten weapons firing at once. Even if you were wearing earphones, the sound of ten trainees firing sophisticated weapons at once was tremendous. And in clandestine operations, reacting to something the wrong way was bad enough, but reacting to something you weren't even supposed to know was going to happen could mean blowing your cover—and ending your life.

"Fire!" the instructor commanded.

Without thinking, Michael squeezed off five rounds. In earlier sessions, he had been hampered by too much thinking, instinctively trying to assess what wrist position and stance would yield the most bullets in the center mass they were all aiming for. That method had yielded a pattern on the dummy like a pool table after a good break. This time he was sure he had managed to rack those balls together.

Michael leaned down to pick up the shells he had scattered and saw that over his right shoulder, the instructor had pressed the button to bring up his sheet. It whizzed to a stop in front of them.

"Well, he ain't goin' ta the pitcher show tonight, that's fer sure," the instructor drawled, lightly tapping the human form outlined on the stiff paper with his grizzled knuckles. Right in the center of the chest, as Vaughn had hoped, were the majority of the holes. As the instructor moved on to the next student, Vaughn suppressed a small grin. It had taken all the trainees some time to decode this instructor's West Texas accent, but Vaughn was almost sure that he had just been given a compliment.

If only I could take out the bad guys with my hockey stick, Vaughn thought. *The CIA would just have to make a commitment to only send me to places like Finland, and I'd be in business.*

Even though he wasn't really sure what a "pitcher show" was, Vaughn was happy to get any acknowledgment that wasn't an instructor leaning over to flip a piece of equipment the right way or—even worse—saying "Absolutely not" to one of his conjectures in class. He was starting to understand that compliments—any form of reassuring human communication, in fact—were rare in this new world.

"Great job, Vaughn!" his fellow trainee Nick Pastino cried, giving him a big, fake smile. Then Nick smirked and spat a big mouthful of tobacco near Vaughn's shoes—making sure, as usual, that the instructor was too far away to witness it.

This time, Vaughn managed not to jump back, just as he had when shooting. If you hung around

Pastino enough, you realized he only came right up to the line—he never dared cross it.

Although it had only been six months, it seemed that at least six years, possibly an entire decade, had elapsed since the blank-faced man in the wrinkled gray suit had finally come to get him. Since then he had been bussed over from Langley to the campus-like Farm, where all career trainees in the CIA learned how to find, recruit, and handle spies.

So far, his time at the Farm had been everything Vaughn had expected it would be. He was in his CIA-issued garb, picking locks, engaging in CIA role-playing sessions, and taking what seemed like triple his college course load. What he hadn't expected was the incredible rush he got from it all.

"Jump!" the instructors shouted. "Fire!" "Release!" "Abort!" Vaughn obeyed every directive with gusto, throwing himself into every exercise, and he loved them all.

In addition, Vaughn felt the security that came from doing something he knew he was truly good at. Although he'd always enjoyed his academic work, he was glad to find that his dread of being doomed to a job behind a desk at some podunk university had been well founded. Vaughn had always been sure that something would be missing in the academic career his professors urged him towards—that he could never be happy just lecturing students, correcting papers, and then pulling into the driveway of his suburban split-level at six o'clock. He didn't know why he'd been so sure that a career at the CIA would fill that hole, but now that he found himself perfectly at home disassembling the latest firearms, flipping a fellow trainee onto the mat, and discussing signals technology, he was glad that he'd been right.

Right about everything, that is, except for one important aspect: what pains in the neck some of his fellow trainees might turn out to be.

Even though the company line at the Farm was that you were only competing with yourself, in fact, it was more like a huge family. The instructors were the parents, and the trainees were the brothers and sisters. Except this was no volleyball game at a campground. These were special brothers and sisters: siblings who got to race real cars, drive state-of-the-art speedboats, and parachute out of honest-to-God airplanes.

And like all families, it had its black sheep.

Vaughn didn't even bother to shoot a look back at Pastino. He and his fellow recruits had tacitly agreed to use the same method with the difficult team member: freeze him out when they could and tolerate him when they couldn't.

Their unity on the subject of Pastino was the one thing that made him bearable. Because Vaughn and his fellow CT's had all had the same reaction to Nick that first day they'd all arrived: instant hatred.

His first day, Vaughn had arrived at Langley at seven A.M. sharp, his bags packed only with essentials, per the instructions given to him by Les. A serious young man with a clipboard had taken Vaughn's things and ushered him into a small room off the main lobby of the vast, sprawling megalith that was the CIA's main headquarters in Langley, Virginia.

There were already some recruits seated around the table. "Well, if it isn't Michael Vaughn," one of them burst out. Happily surprised, Michael saw that it was Akiko Schwartz.

"Hey," he said, coming forward to clasp her hands, this time prepared to fight back with a strong shake of his own.

"Don't worry—I've cut down on my reps," Akiko said, giving him just one firm shake, then releasing him.

"Not quite enough," Michael winced, laughing.

Like any group of strangers suddenly thrust

upon one another, the assembled men and women went around the table and introduced themselves. In addition to Akiko and Vaughn, there was Don Hewitt, a slightly portly aeronautical engineer and former pilot in the air force; Chloe Murphy, a baby-faced twenty-three-year-old wunderkind with a Ph.D. in linguistics; Melvin Brewer, a former police detective and lieutenant in the army; and Sam Ortiz, a helicopter pilot and former high-school physics teacher.

As Vaughn looked around at his future team-mates, his jitters turned to excitement. All of them seemed intelligent and interesting—so far, at least, good people to be stuck with. He also noticed that they already appeared to be in sync in one significant way. Everyone's hair was freshly cut—the women's to chin-length, the men's to just above the collar—and they were all dressed in corporate casual—khakis and plain button-downs. *Either we're already on the same wavelength,* Vaughn thought, *or the CIA has one hell of a subliminal fashion directive going.*

"My name is Betty Harlow," a woman announced, striding into the room. Vaughn realized with shock that it was the folksinger lady from his final interview. She was not quite as tall as he'd thought, Vaughn saw, and she walked with a slight limp, gripping a dark, shiny wooden cane for support as she gazed around at the trainees.

The chatter had died down the minute she'd entered the room, and the small measure of comfort the trainees had built up from friendly conversation evaporated completely. Now that Betty Harlow was in the room, they all seemed to be thinking this wasn't just a dream anymore—the job they'd worked so hard to attain was actually going to start. But those tests they'd passed, the interrogations they'd sat through, the physical challenges they'd overcome were only the beginning. Now that it was down to the wire, were they going to have what it took to make it through CIA training?

As if she'd read their minds, Betty smiled. It wasn't an entirely nice smile. "You've all done well enough to be chosen for the career trainee program at the CIA," she said, measuring out her words so that each fell like a successive weight on a bar. "Now we'll see if you can do well enough to actually work for the CIA."

Suddenly, there was a loud bang. They all jumped—even Betty Harlow. The group had been assembled for at least twenty minutes, and Vaughn had assumed that those at the table made up the entirety of their training team. However, a new member had loudly thrown open the door to their room. Wearing sunglasses, espadrilles, and a violently orange Hawaiian shirt, the man they would come to know as Nick Pastino staggered—and that was definitely the word, *staggered*—into the room.

"Whose butt do I have to kick to get a cup of coffee around here?" Nick asked, grinning broadly at his seated classmates and Betty. Then he pounded on his chest like a frat boy and belched.

Vaughn felt as if he and his fellow trainees might actually shatter like glass figurines from the explosion created by Nick's entrance. He found himself fighting the impulse to get up and toss the man from the room like a bouncer at an exclusive bar.

But he stopped himself. *This isn't a bar,* Vaughn thought. *And if there's anyone who really doesn't need your help with a thug, it's one of the top officers at the Directorate of Operations at the CIA.*

Vaughn looked at his fellow trainees to gauge their reactions. Sam and Melvin seemed to be fighting impulses similar to his own. Don looked like he wanted to hide under the table. Chloe just looked horrified. Akiko was harder to read: She was staring at the intruder with almost friendly interest, as if he were some rare specimen of bug in a glass slide.

After the initial shock of his entrance, Betty seemed to have decided to remain unfazed. "Take a seat," she said shortly, as if these kinds of goings-on were beneath her notice. But her order fell on deaf ears. The man had already taken the seat closest to the door and was leaning back in it as if he were about to watch the evening news. He removed a yogurt lodged precipitously in the pocket of his shirt and, finding himself without a spoon, took off the plastic cover and began to slurp it straight from the container.

"As I was saying . . . ," Betty continued, but Vaughn found it hard to pay attention to her. Like a baby or an especially rowdy dog, the man simply sucked all the attention from the room as forcefully and grossly as he sucked the yogurt from the container.

"These packets contain your administrative orders for the next week. When we complete these sets of forms, we will make our way to the facility where you will be doing the majority of your training. Laptops and firearms will be issued. . . ."

Vaughn saw that the young man—his name tag read NED—who had taken his bags had returned. He was passing out folders to each of the trainees with their names stamped across the front, above the CIA logo. The folders were each as thick as a meatball hoagie: They seemed to have been stuffed with about a ream of paper.

"More forms," Akiko muttered, sending Sam into a laughing fit he tried dutifully to suppress. Vaughn found himself on the verge of laughter, too—the shock of the man's entrance, followed by his devoted yogurt-sucking, had made them initially hugely tense, then suddenly punchy.

As each trainee removed a pen from the file and began to settle down to what looked like business as usual, Vaughn gave the man one last glance. The man was twirling in his seat, holding his folder to the overhead light as if it might contain see-through documents. He continued leaning back and then, just on the verge of tipping over, came forward with a loud thump. His folder sliced back against the table, sending a cascade of papers to the floor, which was soon joined by the contents of Chloe's and Don's folders as he swept them over the side as well in an awkward attempt to secure his fluttering pages against the leg of the table.

This time, Betty could not look away. As if it were all too much to bear, she simply walked out of the room. Ned stood watching for a moment, as if he was considering helping out with the mess, then thought the better of it and followed suit.

"Brilliant," Don barked in their wake, his sarcasm clipping the word. He slapped his hands down on the table for emphasis. Vaughn knew it wasn't his folder that had just been messed up, but he wasn't sure he was crazy about this guy, either.

"Here, I'll help you," Melvin muttered, kneeling down by Chloe, who was fruitlessly trying to separate three sets of forms that seemed to have been joined into one increasingly messy heap. "Let's use mine as a guide to put them back in the right order, okay?" Akiko said, beginning to reassemble the forms Chloe had been able to return to the tabletop. Sam joined her in reshuffling, and Vaughn kneeled down with Chloe and Melvin to bring the pile of papers back up to semiorganized groups.

"Seriously, do you know where I can get some coffee around here?" Nick asked, leaning under the table to look at his fellow trainees, all stooping on the floor to clear up the mess he had made.

No one bothered to answer him.

* * *

Michael knew from his research that working as an instructor at the Farm was one of the most coveted appointments at the CIA. Only the most experienced and effective personnel were asked to take six months, one year, or two years off to bring the next generation of intelligence officers into the fold.

Betty Harlow, he was learning, was the crème de la crème of CIA intelligence. She'd been intimately involved in the end of the Cold War and the fall of the Iron Curtain, and then with operations in the Balkans and the rest of Eastern Europe. Her work had toppled puppet dictators in South America and brought arms brokers in the Middle East to justice. In short, she was no one to mess with.

As she walked down the winding, collegiate paths of the Farm, trainees and instructors fell into a practically reverent silence until her cane had thumped by. She had not yet taught Vaughn's team directly, but she was a shadowy presence throughout all of their training. She would suddenly appear at the classroom door during ballistics training or join them in the screening room as they watched tapes made from hidden cameras of their operations in the Vault, a nearly mile-long network of waterways and caves, or Main Street, the re-creation of a city street that the trainees used in many of their role-playing situations. She never added to the instructor's comments, Vaughn noticed, but he got the idea that she was keeping pretty close tabs on every trainee.

Which all helped to explain why, as a team, they had decided to stay mum about Nick Pastino.

Although the seven-member team had instructors in everything from dead-drops to disguises, officially, Betty was their team's reviewing officer. And while Ned was supposed to exist in an ombudsman capacity, none of them could really imagine going up to the poker-faced young man to complain that they thought one of their team members was a vile, stupid bully.

They'd discussed it as a group almost the first chance they'd gotten, right after they'd sat through the first official day of training at the Farm, a series of lectures by all their instructors on how teamwork was the core principal of the CIA.

"Take a look at the other people in this room," one of their instructors had warned. "Get to know them well, because we aren't going to be the ones training you, okay? They are."

"When you're out in the field, the only thing you can depend on is your team," another had emphasized. "If you can't work with a team while you're training, you won't be able to work for the CIA."

That night before dinner, they had all found themselves—*sans* Nick—in the common room at the end of the hallway of the dorm where they were housed with three other classes. "So, I guess they want us to work together as a team, huh?" Chloe had joked, breaking the ice.

Akiko leaned over and switched off the TV, which had been set to the all-news station. Another class of trainees who had already been there for a few months came down the stairs, presumably on their way to dinner. The two groups exchanged waves, and once she was sure they were gone, Akiko spoke. "We've got to talk. And I think you all know about what."

Melvin leaned back in one of the fuzzy, mushy-seated chairs that seemed to proliferate in the common rooms of every building in the Farm. The instructors' digs, Vaughn assumed, were a little more posh. "I don't know," Melvin said, shaking his head. "It's only the first day. Every speech has been about working together, and we're ganging up on the poor guy already."

"Poor guy," Don snorted. "He's a complete idiot."

Chloe waved her hands dismissively. "It's not necessary to get nasty," she said. "I think we just have to agree that, for now, we're all aware that there might be a problem."

"Might be?" Akiko snorted. "That seems like a generous statement."

"I agree with Chloe," Sam broke in. "If we just know for now that we're aware of it, that seems to be enough."

"To tell you the truth," Melvin said, "at this point, I'm not sure I'm really comfortable having this conversation. It seems like any conversation we're going to have about Nick should probably involve Nick."

Vaughn leapt in. "Listen, this is classic. My girlfriend's a psychology major, and she's always talking about this stuff. In group dynamics, there are certain personalities that thrive on . . . disrupting the order of the group."

"So you're saying we should do something?" Sam asked warily. The others in the group looked suddenly cautious too, as if Vaughn had suggested they take Nick out like a band of vigilantes.

Vaughn laughed. "No, just the opposite. I just meant, whatever he's doing, it's working. You see how he's got us fighting amongst ourselves and not trusting each other already?"

Melvin was nodding fiercely. "That's what I mean. We have to stay cool. We can't go running around like a bunch of crybabies. The army is full of bad apples—you just have to work around them. Believe me, they'll split a group apart, and when it gets down to the wire, they don't get the blame for whatever happens, you do."

They were all nodding. "So we're agreed?" Akiko asked in a manner Vaughn was sure had had lawyers on the other side of the table from her quaking in their boots for years. He was impressed that Akiko, who clearly had more experience than any of them in making other people see the wisdom of her point of view, wasn't leaping into the leadership role. In fact, no one was—they were all taking advice and opinions from each other and coming to decisions together. Like people who'd known each other for longer than a day or two. Like a team.

"Wait and see what happens?" Akiko reiterated, looking around at all the faces. Vaughn gave his yes with the rest.

* * *

As the weeks went by, however, it became clear that the wait-and-see approach had its drawbacks.

The first half of their training, as their instructors had emphasized, was team based and involved the basics of clandestine intelligence work: what their instructors called field tradecraft. "You're going to be spotting, assessing, and approaching your assets," one of their instructors droned, explaining how the team would find people the CIA called NOCs— those under nonofficial cover. These would be personnel in various corporations and agencies that they, as handlers, would train and protect as acquired intelligence for the CIA. "You're going to learn self-defense. You're going to learn to use disguises and provide disguises to others. You're going to learn all about clandestine photography and how to sketch a situation. You're going to learn how to write CIA reports. And at the end of the day, PDR is what you're going to do. Procure. Document. Report."

It was all pretty straightforward, except that Nick seemed preternaturally skilled in throwing a wrench in whatever operations they were performing. As they went through their training in self-defense, for example, Nick seemed to take particular pleasure in slamming Chloe, the least powerful in the group, to the mat. Once, Vaughn could have sworn he'd seen him grind his elbow into her spine as he locked her into a submission pose.

"You okay?" Vaughn asked her after she'd tapped out and Nick had released her. Chloe had walked away from the group to the side mats they used for their stretches, and she was leaning over as if she was in pain. "Fine," Chloe answered through gritted teeth. Vaughn could see tears standing out in her eyes. He'd seen what Nick had done—how could the instructor have missed it?

He was hoping he'd be called on to spar with Nick next, but the instructor called Akiko to the line. She didn't even bother to do the preliminary assessment. In a second, Nick was slammed on his face, his elbow held back to the breaking point by Akiko, who hadn't even mussed her ponytail.

Nick tapped the mat. "Give!" he finally burst out, his voice muffled by the plastic padding in his face.

Akiko got up slowly, taking her time releasing Nick's arm. Nick jumped to his feet, glaring. "Ortiz," the instructor called blandly, motioning him to come spar with Akiko. Their teacher hadn't noticed anything, and they all, it seemed, let out a collective breath.

On the one hand, Vaughn knew, it was satisfying watching Akiko kick butt on behalf of one of their teammates. But on the other hand, he knew that what the instructors kept repeating was true: They were here to teach each *other.* That was the way it worked in the field, and there wasn't room for anything else. If they were all protecting each other from and wreaking revenge on one person, they weren't working together. They weren't supposed to have real enemies; they were supposed to take turns being the enemy, teammate, and asset for each other. If they were all focusing on Nick, they had no time to learn from and teach each other.

"Oomph!" Ortiz said, his face also ground into the mat. Akiko had slammed him, but not as harshly. They were all doing that—using the energy they needed for one another to defeat Nick.

"Bitch," Nick muttered as the instructor gave Sam some directions and Akiko watched, nodding. Vaughn whipped his head around. He couldn't believe what he'd heard.

"Yeah," he heard Melvin mutter back. "It's a bitch that you can't beat her, champ."

Vaughn breathed, trying to let his rage out slowly. His heart was racing, and his temper was up. But if Melvin could keep himself from getting physical with Nick, he reasoned, well, then, so could he.

It would have been easier on all of them if Nick had been incompetent—if his performance had been as poor as his personality. But the hard truth was that he excelled both in the field and the classroom. His shooting trumped everyone's except Melvin's, and his performance in their role-playing asset acquiring, scoping out dead-drops, and performing nighttime clandestine maneuvers always got a special nod from the instructor. The demented mentality he'd revealed in the conference room that first day at Langley was totally absent in the classrooms too—as Nick discussed how to analyze and sift through complex information to learn what was disinformation, what was chatter, and what was real in a variety of international scenarios, even Vaughn was impressed.

But that didn't make up for how Nick was always breezing into their dorm at two or three in the morning, loud and obnoxious, or teasing and berating slow Don on the three-mile runs they took at five A.M. every day. Somehow, although his behavior seemed brazen and openly destructive to the team, the instructors either didn't notice or had given Nick a free pass. To them—and they were the ones who mattered—Nick was just one of the team. Vaughn and the others kept assuming that one of the instructors would notice Nick's antics and shut him down. But the lip service they gave to students only competing with themselves was definitely true in one respect. And in that regard, it was clear that they all felt that Nick was a particularly valuable member of the team—his team of one.

Vaughn started to think back over all the things Nick had done since they'd come to the Farm. It was true: As isolated incidents, they would all seem fairly minor—a joke about Don that could have just been in bad taste, a physical move toward Chloe that could have just been a misjudging of strength. Taken together, however, they added up to a veritable siege, a kind of psychological warfare. Was the troublemaking deliberate on Nick's part, Vaughn wondered, or merely instinctive? Did he have any idea what he was doing to the group, and, if so, what was his purpose in messing with them? Was he some genius who knew that if he distracted his team members, he'd come out on top—or was he just a naturally obnoxious idiot who was getting the better of six formerly mild-mannered, successful people?

Nora could help me out with sorting through this guy's m.o., Vaughn suddenly thought. *That is, if I were allowed to talk to her about what goes on here.*

Vaughn remembered a phrase from his reading about the history of the CIA. The phrase came from James Angleton, the agency's former head of counterintelligence, and it referred to what he'd perceived as the Soviets' campaign of disinformation to their American enemies. They were propagating, he'd said, "a wilderness of mirrors."

And now I'm in the wilderness of mirrors of the Farm, Vaughn thought.

At the far corner of the gym, something caught the corner of Vaughn's eye. It was Betty, standing against the tall white walls, perfectly silent, somehow almost blending in to the background. How long had she been standing there? Vaughn wondered.

And even more important, had she been able to see what the instructors had all been missing?

* * *

That evening, Vaughn caught up on his e-mail. The Farm's computer network allowed him to send blind e-mails, and he'd been sending occasional messages to his mother supposedly from the University of Geneva—although, as she confessed the technology was beyond her, the wait for a reply could be considerable. Usually the only mail in his box besides replies from her were additional paperwork from his instructors, schedule changes, or administrative notices. The e-mail he found that night, however, was personal.

To: vaughn@etu.unige.ch

From: ncarlisle@columbia.edu

Dear Michael,
I got this address from your mother. It's been awhile, hasn't it? I've been so busy I haven't

even had a chance to think, but I have a lot to tell you—about my program, about everything. Are you going to be back in the States anytime soon?

Je te manque beaucoup, chéri—

Nora

Michael's heart was in his throat. He wanted to laugh at Nora's use of French; the language she had avowed even *sounded* like snails rolling around on china (bad enough that French people ate them). He was so glad that Nora had finally gotten in touch with him, he wanted to shout with relief. But her letter posed a problem.

Now he'd have to write her back.

5

"I'VE GOT AN IDEA," Akiko said, smoothing her neat hair back under her baseball cap.

The group of recruits—Sam, Melvin, Chloe, Don, Akiko, and Vaughn—were enjoying what had become their weekly routine: burgers and fries in the Farm's canteen, the wood-paneled retreat that functioned as bar and eatery for all the CTs and the Farm personnel when they couldn't stand the cafeteria one more day. Even though the seven-member team spent all their time together in classes and performing mock operations, these dinners served as a break from regular study groups and mealtimes—a chance to discuss issues, events, and of course, problems. And although they'd tried to get Nick to come in the beginning, he'd refused. Whenever he wasn't required to be with them, he disappeared to someplace where the team couldn't find him—into the camp's acres of woodland to hang out with his wild-animal buddies, Vaughn suspected.

"Spill it," Melvin said, licking the ketchup that had squeezed out of his overstuffed burger onto his thumb.

Vaughn stuffed a few of the commissary's sadly soggy fries in his mouth and looked around at his fellow team members. In the months they'd been at the Farm, they'd all become noticeably different: certainly fitter, more alert, yet also somehow quieter and more self-contained. Melvin, who'd already had rock-hard abs and a soldier's demeanor, now seemed even more coolly judicious. Sam's jittery edge had been shaved off, and he was like a panther—coiled, dangerous, ready to spring. Chloe's hesitation was gone, and she went into spectacular 180-degree turns on speedboats and cars without fear, once even toppling Nick with a sharp cut to the windpipe during their sparring sessions. Akiko, like Melvin, seemed to have risen to a new level of physical and mental expertise. Even Don seemed taller.

And how have I changed? Vaughn wondered. *If I asked them, what would my teammates say about me?*

He knew he *felt* like a pretty different person. The worried, sometimes almost self-pitying boy of some months before was gone, and his last name had somehow taken the place of his first. Now he felt almost like Batman sometimes, as if his new knowledge had given him special powers. When he shadowed Chloe or Sam in their exercises, he could actually picture himself on a real city street in some foreign city tailing an asset or setting up an operation. Patiently explaining to an instructor what it would mean to procure information for the U.S. government during a role-play, he found himself so caught up in his argument that he became almost impatient—when would he be allowed to put his powers to real use? And parachuting out onto a field from a military cargo plane during their paramilitary training, then returning and spending all night in the library with his team writing and transmitting a cable—the raw field reports officers were required to file from operations—he felt a kind of mastery that even his greatest shot in a hockey or pool game had never given him.

Overall, the entire team had come closer to the

CIA ideal: someone who could perform both complex physical *and* psychological feats. Or, in one instructor's words, a person who could get out of anywhere and talk anyone into anything.

"Is your plan to get this place to stock some Dr Pepper?" Chloe asked Akiko, slurping her Pepsi mock-angrily. "Because I'm dying over here."

"Why don't you just bring some in on the weekends and put it in the dorms?" Vaughn asked, grinning. "Don't you have a Ph.D., lady?"

Chloe glared, then slitted her eyes toward Don, who was absorbed in his eggplant parmigiana. "I *have* been bringing it into the dorms," she said sotto voce. "It keeps liberating itself from the area of the refrigerator."

Don suddenly looked up, as if he'd just now tuned into the conversation. "Hey, is it you who's been bringing in the Dr Pepper?" he asked, reaching across to pat Chloe on the shoulder. "Thanks a lot, man."

Chloe's voice rose to a shriek. "I'm going to kill you!" she said, crumpling her napkin and preparing to launch an assault.

Akiko's voice cut smoothly through the melee. "So, anyway, about my idea," she said loudly. Chloe lofted the napkin gently over Don's head, then settled back in her seat to listen.

"It has to do with Nick," Akiko continued. A collective groan rose from around the table, Vaughn's voice the loudest of all.

They'd debated Nick endlessly, but after a few stalemates, the final decision had been made: There was nothing they could do about him. Though he was continuing to drive them crazy, he was their instructors' favorite, and he hadn't done anything big enough for them to pin on him. In short, it was a strictly slash-and-burn operation at this point.

Vaughn was especially sensitive about reopening the Nick issue. Since that day he'd been spat at by Nick at the firing range, things had only deteriorated, and an event had occurred that had almost caused Vaughn to be ejected from training altogether.

The evening of that day at the shooting range, after a particularly brutal end-of-the-day five-K run an instructor had surprised them with, the group had been straggling back to the dorm. Vaughn was walking a little ahead of the group, trying to stretch, when out of nowhere, Nick brushed past him, clipping him so roughly that Vaughn almost fell to his knees.

"Hey," Vaughn called out after him angrily, not caring if the instructor heard. In fact, he was hoping he would, so they could have a public confrontation and sort this out. He was hot, he was tired, and he had had enough.

But Nick had sprinted far ahead, and he wasn't stopping. "Hey!" Vaughn yelled again, taking off after him. Leaving the rest of the group in the dust, he reached Nick's side. And as they pounded the ground side by side, he couldn't help himself: He reached out to give Nick's shoulder a shove.

They had run so far that they'd made it from the clearing where they usually finished out the runs into a sparsely wooded area a few hundred yards behind the dorm. "What do you want, golden boy?" Nick asked, giving Vaughn a manic grin and performing a sweep-kick so quickly that Vaughn found himself on his back before he even knew what was happening.

Vaughn got to his feet quickly, but not quickly enough. Nick had already reached the patio of the dorms. When Vaughn raced over to tackle him at the knees, they fell to the cracked concrete surface like two tons of bricks.

"What the hell are you doing?" Nick screamed, trying to push Vaughn off him. Vaughn reached out to try to pin him, but Nick continued to land painful punches on his most vulnerable areas, his kidneys and windpipe, all the while continuing to scream as if he were being torn apart by a pack of hyenas.

Vaughn finally managed to catch Nick's arm and twist it behind him. Under the floodlights, they tussled, Vaughn struggling to catch Nick's arms to stop his painful jabs as the rest of the group emerged, running, from the darkness of the woods.

Suddenly Nick went limp with Vaughn sitting on top of him, and Vaughn's arms, which had been tangled up with Nick's, flew free to deliver a knockout punch to the side of Nick's head. Nick turned his head to the side and groaned.

Vaughn could hear both the instructor's voice and Nick's over the din. ". . . wasn't doing anything . . . Sonofabitch just tackled me. . ." and a harsh "Break it up, now, boys, break it up!" He felt Melvin's arms pulling him off Nick while he watched, feeling almost disembodied, as the instructor kneeled down to check on his fallen opponent.

"He just tackled me!" Nick was still screaming as he got slowly to his feet, holding his now bloody nose with one hand and pointing at Vaughn with the other. The instructor looked at Vaughn, then at Nick, then back at Vaughn. The rest of the group kept looking between the two men. Vaughn was trying to figure out how Nick had gotten that bloody nose. When he'd tackled him? He didn't remember landing any direct blows except for that last punch at the head, and that had been an accident.

"He slammed into me," Vaughn finally heard himself say calmly. "He slammed into me, and I was just trying to catch up with him so that we could talk."

"Talk?" Nick yelled indignantly, the sweatshirt sleeve he was holding up to the gushing pipe of his nose becoming increasingly bloody. "Dude, you're out of your mind. Does this look like we've been *talking*?"

Vaughn suddenly caught a glimpse of himself in the dorm's windows. While Nick looked like he'd been through a couple of rounds with a helicopter, his face and hands bloody, his knees cut, and his clothes disheveled and ragged, Vaughn looked barely touched—like he'd been on a long run and through a field of wildflowers, which was actually pretty close to the truth.

Was he *so* filled with rage that he'd been able to beat Nick so badly in so short a time without even noticing what he was doing?

"Son," the instructor said, reaching out toward Vaughn. "I think you'd better cool down and come with me."

Vaughn felt his anger and fear—which had been hovering somewhere around the top of his throat—suddenly plunge down to his gut. Had he really snapped? *I could be thrown out of training for this,* Vaughn thought. People who lost their tempers had no place at the CIA. But how could he have beaten Nick that badly? He'd just meant to slow him down, to get in his face, to make him finally talk about what he'd been doing.

Maybe I don't belong here after all, he found himself thinking, looking at the bloody and battered Nick.

"Wait," Akiko broke in. "It's been a tense day for all of us. We've developed a way to deal with problems as a team, sir," she said, turning to the instructor, "and I'd appreciate it if you'd let us try to work this out among ourselves before you took this anywhere else."

The instructor hesitated, then looked at the rest of the team. "That so?" he asked, looking into all of their faces carefully.

Sam, Chloe, Melvin, and Don all looked at Akiko, then at each other. Slowly, they turned back to the instructor. They all nodded.

Vaughn looked at Nick, waiting for him to burst

out again, scream that it wasn't true, that they had no system for dealing with problems. But Pastino only stood with the blood running onto his shirt, a look of menace and anger on his face.

Well, I guess Nick is scared of something, Vaughn thought. *He knows he can fool our instructors, but he also knows that if this goes to a disciplinary hearing, his career would be at risk too.*

Vaughn was glad to have finally found the limits of Nick's playacting. However, he didn't need Nick to try this poor-me routine in front of Betty Harlow. It was scary enough that he'd provoked Vaughn the way he had.

The instructor was still looking at the group. "Work it out," he finally said. "Work it out quickly, or we'll work it out for you."

"I'll let you know, sir," Akiko said calmly. Not for the first time, Vaughn gave a silent prayer of thanks for her powers of persuasion.

The instructor walked off. When he was finally out of earshot, Nick started laughing. Vaughn couldn't believe what he was hearing.

"Nice work, guys," he said, shaking his head. He stuck his hands in his sweatshirt pockets, positively happy now, and disappeared inside the dorms.

"Psycho," Chloe said, watching him leave. She

turned to Vaughn. "Vaughn, what happened? What's going on?"

Vaughn looked at their faces, each a mix of sympathy and worry. Vaughn knew they were wondering why he'd beaten Nick so badly—and he knew he'd scared them by doing so. The thing was, he'd also scared himself.

"I don't exactly know," he began.

*   *   *

Since that day, Nick's antics had decreased, but the wall of ice that had gone up between him and his teammates was making them all suffer. In their weekly reports, they'd all seen their assessments go down. It was unavoidable—they were supposed to work as a team, and they weren't doing so. But while they were all thrown off balance by Nick's presence, he seemed to function smoothly and without errors, blocking them out when he had to and working with them when it suited his purposes.

Although Vaughn didn't like the stress he and the rest of the group were under—and he certainly didn't like his assessments going south—lying low and just dealing with it seemed like the best solution. Now Akiko was trying to bring up the problem again. And this time, it could put them all in the same vulnerable situation he'd been in.

"Akiko, do we really need to do this?" Vaughn asked.

Akiko looked at him and nodded. Vaughn sighed.

"My daughter is four," Akiko said, stealing some of Sam's fries, "and she's at that stage where she sometimes tries to play my husband and me against each other."

"Fascinating," Don said, taking a swig of his soda. "You know us childless lugs always like to hear about the little tykes."

"Anyway," Melvin broke in. "Go on, Akiko."

"Well, last time I went home on weekend leave, we decided to try something new to make sure we didn't have another three-chocolate-sundaes-in-one-day situation," she said. Sam laughed, and Akiko gave him a warning glance. "Just bear with me," she said.

"So you punished her and sent her to her room," Don threw in.

Akiko shook her head. "We tried that, but it just seemed to make things worse. She kept picking on her little brother, you know, and it was tantrum city any time we went out in public."

"Sounds like someone we know," Melvin said.

Akiko nodded. "So this time, we decided to do exactly the opposite. If she asked for one candy bar, she got two. She said her brother was bothering her, we sent him to his room. We took her to Great Adventure, got her six videos, let her eat all the candy and popcorn she wanted."

"And she was in heaven," Chloe said. Vaughn thought it sounded like a likely outcome, too.

Akiko shook her head. "She was practically in a coma by the end of the day," she said. "She'd made herself sick with all the Cokes and candy, and she didn't want to watch any of the videos. A friend was supposed to sleep over, and we had to call her and cancel. When we put her to bed, she said, 'I'm tired of this party, Mommy.'" Akiko laughed and shook her head.

"I don't get it," Vaughn asked. "You think we should shut Nick down by giving him too much ice cream?"

Akiko got the same artful look she'd had when she first met Vaughn at the conference. "We've tried freezing him out, kicking his butt, and turning the other cheek," she said. "But we haven't yet tried killing Nick Pastino with kindness."

* * *

The next morning, the Excel schedule on Vaughn's laptop indicated they were starting the day with a two-mile swim, then, after breakfast, doing role-play on Main Street. The day would end with operations against two other teams in the Vault.

"Perfect," Vaughn said, turning the computer off. A day spent mostly in the classroom wouldn't give them much chance to put their plan into action, but work in the field would let them try everything they'd brainstormed the night before.

"Do you think this will actually work?" Chloe had asked as the group went back out into the summer evening.

"We've got enough firearms and demolitions in our coursework," Melvin said. "I think it's a good idea to try to turn down the volume as much as we can."

That morning, at the water's edge, Vaughn saw Don heading over to Nick. It looked like the plan was already taking effect.

Vaughn watched the two men talking from afar, not able to see the confused expression he was sure was on Nick's face. Akiko walked up to his side, trying to rub the goose bumps off her arms in the chilly morning air. "Is it happening?" she asked, giving Vaughn a delighted smile.

"Yup," Vaughn said. Don and Nick had waded into the water, and Don was gesturing wildly. Suddenly, he reached up to Nick, grabbed him, and pulled him down into the water with him. "Is this the right way?" Vaughn could hear carrying faintly over the water as the two men floated off in a strange grapple of a backstroke.

"Let's just see if he can keep it up," Akiko said.

In Vaughn's opinion, Don more than did his job. He peppered Nick with questions throughout the swim, leading the instructor to comment on the situation—thankfully, with approval. "Looks like Don's really shaping up!" he said to Vaughn, cutting cleanly through the water as he observed his students. "I'm glad to see him taking some initiative."

At breakfast, phase II went into action. Chloe and Akiko hadn't eaten breakfast with Nick since one early week in the program, when they'd unsuccessfully tried to persuade him to stop making himself such a thorn in everyone's sides. But now they joined him as if there had never been a problem. "Hey, Nick, what's your favorite movie?" he heard Chloe say. "Akiko and I were just talking about *The Matrix* trilogy."

Vaughn had to hide his smile in his pint of milk. Akiko's plan might have seemed obvious, but it was also brilliant. Because now, if he wanted some peace, it was Nick who had to stalk off angrily in front of the instructors, not them. And instead of constantly being annoyed and frustrated, they'd reversed the equation—now Nick was trying to swim away from Don, whom he'd previously loved to pick on, and was clearly so terrified that Chloe and Akiko would talk to him, he'd abandoned his eggs and coffee and run for the door.

The problem had been that the team wasn't willing to pay Nick back in kind—to insult him, assault him, risk jeopardizing the operations like Nick routinely did. But there was nothing to stop them from being incredible pests—and acting so nice about it that Nick would have to throw a fit just to get rid of them.

"He's psyching us out," Akiko had said the night before. "So we have to psych him out one better."

Vaughn turned and saw Nick leaving the cafeteria practically at a dead run. Akiko and Chloe had warned that they were going to get into a discussion of the merits of *The Real World* as soon as they could—even though Vaughn knew Akiko had only seen the show half-asleep with her daughter and that Chloe had never seen it at all.

In their first exercises of the day, a slightly more complicated part of the plan had to be put into action. "To get back the power, we've got to give him the power," Akiko had said.

"You sound like Oprah," Melvin laughed.

"I'm serious," Akiko said. "It works. Just let me try it, and you'll see what I mean."

So when it came time to take roles in their operation, Akiko stepped up and said the words none of the rest of them wanted to say. "I think Nick should lead today," she offered.

The instructor looked at her. Since the team always chose its leader, Nick had never functioned in that capacity before. But the instructor was clearly pleased at the idea. "Nick?" she said, then nodded her permission to the group. Nick nodded back at her, then looked at the group as if they'd each sprouted a third arm.

"You've got a midsized company with standard security, both human and online. Your team's job is to hack onto the network, disable the security, and distribute bugs throughout the facility. Mission time's eighteen minutes, pullout by air. Everyone clear? Good." The instructor clicked on her stopwatch, then looked back at the group. "Go."

Nick looked as if he was unclear what to do now that his role was a little more complicated than delivering sarcastic comments under his breath.

"Um . . . Sam and Chloe, hit the network," he finally said, standing up a little straighter. "Melvin and Akiko—get the hump on the door. Don, you're fix-it—maintain the mikes. And Vaughn"—here he looked straight at Vaughn for the first time since their fight—"you're coming with me."

As the team scattered, Vaughn and Nick began to make their way up the exterior of the building, aided by crampons and a sophisticated pulley system used routinely by SWAT teams. They reached the fourth floor of the building without any problems and held their position momentarily while Nick checked in with the team. "We're at the window. Is the system down?" Nick asked via headset.

"Good to go," Vaughn heard Don reply, and Nick pushed open the window and disappeared. Moments later, his arm reappeared, held out as if to give Vaughn a hand inside.

"C'mon!" Vaughn heard Nick yell from inside.

Dangling over the window's ledge, Vaughn hesitated—would Nick do something that would actually endanger his life? He hoped that Akiko was right: that when Nick was in the lead, he had too much heat on him to pull any tricks. As he reached for Nick's arm, Vaughn was relieved to find that she had been right. Nick's grip on Vaughn's arm was steady and sure.

Once inside the facility, Nick and Vaughn hastened to distribute the bugs throughout the fake office. It was a delicate balance—while the bugs had to remain in a central enough position that they could pick up the information needed, placing them out in the open also placed them in jeopardy, where they could be swept aside, thrown away, or—even worse—discovered.

"You ready?" Nick asked as they looked around the room.

"Let's roll," Vaughn said, making his way out of the window first. Back on the ground, they rendezvoused with the technical and ground team, then hooked up with Don.

"Move it out!" Nick hollered at them as the helicopter lowered itself to the landing field. He slapped each of them on the back as they entered the small cab of the helicopter. Vaughn knew the exercise wasn't really over—once the helicopter touched down again, they'd be disembarking, going over every step of the exercise with the instructors, questioning each team member's roles, the choices they'd made, and how well they'd worked. In real operations, they would be writing a cable and sending it to Langley now. Instead, they were just pulling up briefly, then touching down to go get lectured.

But for now, it seemed that Akiko's plans had been a striking success.

As the team left the copter and rejoined the instructor, Melvin and Sam stepped up to do their part. "Dude, can I ask you something?" Vaughn heard Sam ask Nick. "We've got some questions about Friday's lecture—you seemed to have some really good insights. Can we come study with you tonight?"

"Um . . . ," Vaughn heard Nick say. "I was really planning to—"

"C'mon, man, share the wealth!" Melvin chortled. "We're a team, remember?"

Akiko and Vaughn watched them walk off together, then hung back for a second to revel in their triumph with Chloe and Don.

"We gave him the keys to the city," Vaughn said, joining Chloe, Don, and Akiko in a group high-five. "And now it's ours again."

6

VAUGHN ADJUSTED HIS GOGGLES and made sure the oxygen meter on his tank was reading correctly. The team had gotten off surprisingly easily with the instructors that morning, and they'd been given an unprecedented hour off before lunch. Vaughn had spent his happily reading newspapers in three languages on the Internet, secure in the knowledge that Melvin and Sam were tailing Nick like the worst kind of protective detail.

I don't care how well the operation went this morning, Vaughn thought. *I hope they're making him talk about* The Real World *too.*

But now it was afternoon, and the team was assembling for one of their most difficult exercises: a survey course through the Vault.

Of all the complicated exercises that went on at the Farm—racing boats, jumping out of planes, running through training courses in the woods—those that went on in the Vault were the most difficult and the most closely guarded. A two-mile-long network of underwater caves, waterways, tunnels, and derelict structures, it was meant to prepare the trainees for situations no one could foresee: getting out of burning or compromised buildings, working in cities during riots and insurrections, being abandoned in unknown regions. Vaughn likened it to the survival trips he knew some Native American tribes sent adolescents on—except that on the Farm, you worked with a team, and no one had ever stayed in the Vault longer than a day.

That he knew of.

Their team's mission was simply to survey and map out a certain part of the Vault. This was a typical reconnaissance mission, and Vaughn was confident that with the work they'd gotten done this morning on Main Street, they'd come through again with flying colors.

"Vaughn, you'll be leading the team through our maneuvers this afternoon," the instructor said as they buzzed out on the flat-bottomed boat towards one of the Vault's many entrances. Vaughn glanced at his team members, all wearing their scuba gear, their flippered feet dangling in the water. They'd all planned to choose Nick again as team leader, but they could make this work.

"Sounds good," he replied, trying put a hearty tone into his words that he didn't quite feel. In his gear, Nick was unreadable, his half-covered face pointed toward their destination. There was no sign of whether Sam and Melvin's company had sent him over the edge.

This entrance to the Vault required trainees to swim about a hundred yards through an underwater chamber to reach the spot they were required to survey. Vaughn chose Chloe to serve as the lead, then counted the swimmers off. One by one, they flipped backward into the water and made their way to the entrance in a tight line, each swimmer keeping a close eye on the one in front. Vaughn brought up the rear, making sure no one was straggling or getting out of line. In a space this tight, any mistake could cause an underwater traffic jam, leaving the swimmers no way to get in or out.

They reached the underwater cave with no problem, despite Don's slowing the formation slightly during the ten feet or so of rock wall they were forced to climb freehand after depositing their flippers neatly at the bottom. "Okay," Vaughn said after they were all assembled at the top, flipping his mask up and pulling off the watertight pack that held their tools. "I want Chloe and Sam on the south passageway, Akiko and Melvin in the north corridor, and Don staying at the base to coordinate. Nick," he said, looking in the man's eyes, "you're coming with me."

You wanted to keep an eye on me this morning, right? Vaughn thought. *Nick, believe me, I'm keeping an eye on you.*

The team secured their wireless headsets, took their pencil-thin cameras, and set off. The mission was to take as many photos of the area as they could, from which they would later determine the contours and depth of the various regions. Vaughn knew the CIA was working on unmanned drones that could fly over facilities and take the same kind of depth-recording photographs, but they hadn't been given the sophisticated prototypes to play with yet at the Farm.

Cameras were another story. Since he'd arrived at the Farm, Vaughn had seen cameras in every form imaginable: credit cards, pens, even one embedded in a piece of bread in a tuna-fish sandwich. The ones they were using today were strictly utilitarian, though—small clip-ons that fit in the palm of the hand and were virtually indestructible.

Vaughn and Nick set off for the far corridor. "Team one, copy?" he asked, beginning the routine headset check. Sam answered in the affirmative. "Team two?"

"Gotcha, chief," Akiko replied.

"Base?" he asked. There was no reply. He jiggled his headset, hearing only the empty hum of the network. "Base?"

"I'll go check him," Nick said, making as if to return. Vaughn put out his hand to stop him—something was crackling through. "Sorry about that," Don said, sounding as if he'd just run four miles. Vaughn grinned. Although Don had finally been able to run the one and a half miles in nine minutes they were all required to complete, it had taken him about ten tries and three weeks longer than anyone else on the team.

"Acquired?" Vaughn asked the teams, trying to determine if everyone had reached their appointed points.

"Team one in," came the reply, followed by team two's affirmative. Vaughn hefted his bag up over another small wall, then began to climb. This exercise required an additional step—Vaughn would be loading all the photos taken onto a laptop at the scene, making some minor calculations, then sending the intelligence over to another computer at the Farm. Although it was easy work that every team member had mastered long ago, Vaughn had never done it on a dark, wet precipice before—and all in the presence of his biggest enemy.

Nick was standing over Vaughn with his arms folded, watching him set up the small dish and laptop that would, had they really been in the field, enable him to bounce information off satellite dishes thousands of miles away and get information back to Langley in seconds. Vaughn still found it impressive that the computer could shoot the images even a few miles. "Want a hand?" Nick asked, smirking.

"I got it," Vaughn said, watching the laptop come to life with a silent sigh of relief. "Let's do it."

Working quickly, Vaughn and Nick attempted to photograph every aspect of the dance hall-sized cave. They would have been crashing into each other but for the smart fabric of their wet suits, which gave off a dull glow about equal to that of a small lantern. The suits were solar, Vaughn knew, and after absorbing only fifteen minutes of direct sunlight, could, powered by body heat, provide the wearer with up to fifteen hours of light if necessary. And if the wearer needed to become invisible suddenly, the uniform could be turned inside out without any loss of power.

Vaughn wanted to get a shot of a cavernlike depression in the corner. Hunkering down, he edged out as far as he dared on the ledge, then began to shoot. There was some kind of assemblage there that he could just barely make out—had it been placed there on purpose to see if the trainees noticed it? Taking a deep breath, he edged out a little farther.

Suddenly, he felt two hands gripping his legs. Nick's voice came out of the darkness. "You're going a little too far," Nick said. Vaughn could almost see the sneer on his face. "You could get hurt doing that kind of thing, you know?"

The smallest push, Vaughn knew, could send him and his camera careening over the edge. And while a recovery team would find him soon enough, he could be badly injured—or worse—before they managed to do so.

Chloe's voice crackled over the headsets. "Team two's out," she said. "Returning to base."

"Copy that," Vaughn almost shouted into the headset. Nick's hands had given him a yank, all right, but back into the chamber. Now Nick had retreated. Had he decided it was too dangerous to try to injure Vaughn? Or had he merely been messing with him— taking him right up to the edge, literally?

"Team one out," Sam echoed. "Returning to base."

Vaughn scrambled back up the satellite station. Nick was hunched over the computer, frowning. "We've lost the link," he said, looking up at Vaughn without expression.

This wasn't the first time Vaughn had suspected Nick of sabotaging missions he had led. But he'd be damned if he was going to let him destroy this one.

"Get out of my way," Vaughn said, moving behind the laptop. He clicked a few keys. The transmitting bar came up, the signal clear. There was no problem with the link.

Nick was standing over him, laughing. "Psych!" he said, giving his ridiculous hyena.

Vaughn wanted to reach out and shove Pastino over the ledge he'd been sprawled out on minutes ago. He'd gained a measure of self-control since their blowup, though. "Very funny," he said, keeping his tone even only by using every ounce of strength he had. "Now give me a hand with these images."

*　*　*

Vaughn and Nick returned to the group about ten minutes later, the transmittal successfully completed. The rest of the team was suited up, and they silently put on their tanks and packs. *Maybe I was wrong about this guy,* Vaughn thought. *Maybe he's just a got a really stupid sense of humor.*

He revised his thinking minutes later, though. As he brought up the rear of the line in the underwater chamber, he suddenly smacked headfirst into Nick's flippers and found himself jammed up against the ceiling of the chamber, his mouthpiece pushed dangerously away.

This is going too far, he thought, scrambling madly to get his mouthpiece back before his lungs began to feel it and he panicked. *This is endangering the welfare of the team!*

In any operation, the last person—the team leader—was always responsible for those in front. Vaughn knew that, whatever was happening, Akiko, Sam, Melvin, Chloe, and Don should continue to swim to safety, then send a person back in, if necessary. But now he was left to subdue Nick in the confines of this tunnel, and he wasn't sure how much oxygen he had left.

However, as Vaughn replaced his mouthpiece and pushed forward to assess the situation, he realized that the first five team members hadn't swum to safety at all. Don was still hanging back, and it looked like *he* was wrestling with Nick.

Vaughn swam forward and grabbed Nick by the shoulders. As he tried to pull him away from Don,

Nick strong-armed him back, sending him floating up toward the cement ceiling again. In the darkness of the tunnel, it was hard to see what was going on. But he *thought* that he saw Nick rip Don's mouth-piece off, then place it in his own mouth and begin to breath from it.

What's he doing? Vaughn thought, frantically trying to swim back toward the two lashing bodies through the muck they'd kicked up with their wrestling. *Has he totally lost his mind?*

But as he finally reached them, the situation abruptly came to a halt. Nick replaced Don's mouth-piece, broke formation, and kicked off in the direction of the departed team.

Vaughn reached Don and held him up in the water. Through the mask, Vaughn could see that Don's eyes held fear and panic. He wasn't breathing into his mouthpiece, and he looked on the verge of passing out.

Securing Don's head firmly under his arm, Vaughn began to kick off after Nick. It was only a few strokes towards the entrance from the tunnel, then a few kicks to the surface of the water, but Vaughn knew he had to get Don out fast. People didn't breathe properly when they went into shock, and they could drown in just an inch of water.

Kicking powerfully, Vaughn dragged Don past

the rest of the group and broke through the surface into the open air. The boat was only a few yards away, and he hauled Don onto the keel, ripping his mask off and checking for vitals. He was about to begin CPR when Don started spurting out mouthfuls of water, coughing and gagging and screaming all at once.

"He . . . he tried to kill me," he choked, pointing Nick, who was just swimming up to the boat. Don's face was turning from blue to white in the late-afternoon sunlight. The rest of the team boarded the craft, removed their masks, and stood dripping onto the deck in the cold wind.

"That's it," the instructor said, flipping the motor on and turning the boat around like a racing demon. "All of you, report to Harlow's office at oh six hundred."

* * *

Vaughn felt as if he'd been debriefing for at least the past twenty-four hours, although it had only been two at most. Facing him were Betty Harlow and their ballistics instructor, Major Gannett.

"And then CT Pastino held your legs and shoved you forward?" Betty was asking for the twentieth time. Vaughn sighed.

"He didn't shove me forward," he repeated. "He just said that what I was doing was dangerous." The two questioners exchanged glances.

"But this isn't the first time he's done something like that," Vaughn said. "I've seen him be rough physically rough with Chloe, and he's always talking to—"

"Be confident that we will be talking to all of you about you interactions with CT Pastino," Betty interrupted. "Please only refer to those circumstances in which you were directly involved."

Vaughn began again. "Well, there was the fight we had a few weeks ago," he began.

"And explain again why you did not report this incident before?" Betty asked.

Vaughn drew in his breath. "I thought . . . ," he said. "I thought we could work it out between ourselves."

Betty shook her head and made a notation on her pad. Gannett's face was becoming increasingly red.

"Sir, you do understand that this lapse may very well have endangered one of the lives of your fellow CTs?" Gannett blasted. The major had gone through a few variations of this explosion approximately every half hour since the debriefing had begun.

"I understand now," Vaughn repeated. "Believe me, I regret my actions and I understand what I did wrong." Betty shook her head again, then looked at Gannett. She made some inscrutable signal, and Gannett nodded slowly.

"We'll get back to you with our decision," Gannett said. Vaughn stood up and left the room. There was nothing else he could do.

He only hoped this dismissal wasn't a final one.

7

VAUGHN MOVED HIS CURSOR over the last paragraph of the report he'd just completed, checking for omissions and errors one last time. "Akiko, did Historical send over those papers I requested?" he shouted over the cubicle. Akiko's face, now framed by long hair and demure pearl earrings, popped up over the four-foot plastic wall.

"What do I look like, your secretary?" she asked, then disappeared again.

"I wish," Vaughn muttered.

"I heard that!" Akiko shouted, rustling her papers ominously.

Vaughn laughed, but bitterly. Since their graduation from the Farm, he and Akiko were perhaps only marginally more likely to be given a secretary than the guys who picked up Langley's garbage at the end of day.

Instead of bringing the team closer together, the last months of their training at the Farm had only increased each member's feelings of disillusionment. By the time training was complete, Vaughn knew that even though on the outside their team functioned as an efficient, streamlined entity, on the inside each member was only counting the days until he or she could graduate and get away.

For some of the members, the desire to escape was strictly family related. Both Akiko and Melvin were married, and although the CIA didn't make spouses hide the fact that they were in the CIA anymore, the training period put a strain on even the strongest marriages. Chloe's biggest strain was not being able to visit her elderly grandfather, whose health had been steadily worsening in the past couple of months. Sam, whose girlfriend thought he had entered a graduate program in the Virginia area, was eager to move in with her and propose so that he could fill her in on the new direction his life was taking. And Don talked all the time about the nieces and nephews he'd missed visiting during his time at the Farm.

Vaughn had learned all this at their regular Sunday dinners at the canteen, but he hadn't told his teammates what was going on in his own life. While he and Nora had shared a few more e-mails since her initial contact, Vaughn had struggled over what he could and couldn't say under his cover, and the distance he'd felt at their graduation over a year ago seemed to have deepened into a large abyss. Mostly, though, what kept his mouth shut around his colleagues was his shame over the blowback from what he thought of as the Pastino Affair.

After the entire team had suffered through numerous hours of debriefing, Betty and Major Gannett had returned to them with a decision: They would continue their training without Nick Pastino, and the report of the incident and those leading up to it would be recorded as black marks on their records. "The key to teamwork is good communication," Gannett blasted at them in the room where they had assembled to wait for the decision. "And in that area, you all get an F minus."

Akiko was the only one with the courage to ask the question they all wanted answered. "What's going to happen to CT Pastino?" she asked, keeping her voice steady under the hundred-watt glare of Major Gannett and the stone-faced mien of Betty. "Will he be continuing his training with another team?"

Betty didn't even bat an eye. "That information is on a strictly need-to-know basis for now," she said, looking around the room. "Are there any other questions?" she asked.

There weren't.

Although Gannett and Betty seemed to assign some responsibility for the blowup to every team member, Vaughn knew it was mostly his fault. He had erupted with rage at Nick, possibly driving him to his actions that day in the Vault. His teammates had tried to protect him when they'd decided not to take the matter public and he had urged them to keep it quiet. And he'd been leading the team on the day Nick had gone haywire, and thus would have been responsible if Don or anyone had died.

"There's probably more to this than meets the eye," Akiko had said to him as they returned to the dorms, giving him a comforting slap on the back. "Don't take it all on yourself."

But I have to take it on myself, Vaughn had silently argued. *It's my fault, and it's my responsibility.*

And after the team had finished their last operations at the Farm and been given their marching orders, it seemed clear that someone very high up agreed with Vaughn. While Chloe was sent to Paris, Melvin to St. Petersburg, Sam to London, and Don to Azerbaijan, Vaughn was to remain at Langley, working not under the deputy director of operations, as he'd trained for, but as a liaison for that department to the directorate of intelligence, the department that handled all the complex analytical work for the CIA.

I can't believe this, Vaughn had thought, reading the printout carefully again to be sure he hadn't made a mistake. *I've been demoted to an analyst!*

While Vaughn knew that the directorate of intelligence was vital to the work of the CIA, the intensive training he'd just received wasn't necessary to become an analyst in that department. Analysts were basically a higher-paid breed of academic, studying the international communities and leaders Vaughn had written papers on in college in order to provide crucial information to the directorate of operations.

I'm not even an analyst, he realized, scanning the document again. *I'm a* liaison *to an analyst!*

Vaughn had been suddenly filled with white-hot hatred for Betty Harlow. *If it's the last thing I do,* he had thought, picturing her long gray hair, her stony face, and her cane with irritation, *I'm going to show that woman that I'm good enough to be an operations officer at the CIA.*

"Hey, Vaughn, have you ever heard of being a

liaison for the DI?" Akiko had asked, using the general shorthand for the directorate of intelligence as she approached, waving her marching orders in her right hand.

"No," he had answered, his mouth filling with bile. He could understand demoting him, but Akiko as well? She hadn't done anything but be his closest ally on the team. Clearly, in the CIA, your friends could drag you down as well as your enemies. "But I have a feeling we're about to learn all about it."

* * *

Both Vaughn and Akiko tried to take a philosophical view towards their positions, which involved writing and sifting through hundreds of counterintelligence reports and raw intel and which Betty Harlow seemed to have created out of thin air just for them. "I was dreading telling my husband we had to move to Kuwait City anyway," Akiko joked.

"Yeah—maybe Harlow knew we'd miss Washington nightlife," Vaughn threw back.

In reality, there was little time for nightlife or for their families. Both Vaughn and Akiko had the same Weeble-like streak: When you punched them, they wobbled, but they wouldn't fall down. It wasn't, at this point, out of love for the job. Pride and competitive instinct kept them both working overtime, even though Betty, back on detail at Langley, seemed to pay little attention to their work.

"Thanks," she'd say brusquely whenever Vaughn or Akiko provided her with a report or a document she'd requested. *Liaison,* as it turned out, also meant working as a private secretary for Betty.

"You've got to stop working so hard," Akiko told Vaughn near midnight one night, when she was finally calling it quits just as he got his usual second wind.

He looked up, trying to see if she was being sarcastic. He knew that to keep her job on track during this difficult period, Akiko was sacrificing valuable time with her family. But what was working late to him? He was only going home to a one-bedroom apartment filled with unpacked boxes and a fridge crammed with leftover pizza and Chinese. He couldn't even look forward to the occasional message from his mother—he hadn't yet had a chance to hook up the phone, and he forgot to pay his cell phone bill so frequently he kept having to start with a new service and change the number.

"*You're* the one who's working too hard," he said, his fingers momentarily ceasing their manic tapping at the keyboard. "You've got a husband and kids—don't they miss you? I don't mind taking on some of the extra work here if you want time to see them."

Akiko smiled. "David understands," she said. "And so do Blanche and Eugene. But I don't think this is going to last much longer, anyway."

Vaughn pushed back from his desk, suddenly filled with concern. "You're not leaving me, are you?" he said. "Because without you, I swear, I'd be running through these halls in a clown suit ooga-ooging in about a week."

Akiko laughed. "With some of your suits, you're basically doing that anyway, Vaughn," she joked. "But seriously, I didn't mean I was talking about leaving the CIA. I meant just what I said: I don't think that this is going to last much longer."

Now Vaughn was definitely all ears. Had Akiko heard that something about their current situation was about to change? What was going on upstairs? "You think we're going to get canned?" he asked, hoping that whatever tip she'd gotten was just malicious gossip.

Akiko sighed and removed her coat, then pulled her seat into Vaughn's little cubicle. She lowered her voice. "The CIA never fires anyone, Vaughn," she said. "I'm talking about something else. You know how our instructors were always going on about PDR?"

"Procure. Document. Report," Vaughn repeated. "The mantra of the directorate of operations."

"Well, over at the justice department, they had another name for it: LCS," Akiko said.

"LCS?" Vaughn asked, rolling it around on his tongue. "Losers chewing superstitions?"

Akiko laughed. "No," she said. "Though that'd be a good name for us too. LCS stands for lying, cheating, and stealing. What the folks in justice thought CIA officers sometimes got a little too caught up in."

Vaughn was confused. "What are you saying?" he said. "That they think we're liars?"

Akiko shook her head, pulling her coat back on. "No," she said. "Just that office politics can get bad enough just in the real world. But picture what happens when you stick a bunch of people who lie, cheat, and steal for a living in an office."

Vaughn kicked back in his seat, locking his hands behind his head and gazing up at Akiko. "Well, let's say I agree that that's what we're really doing—"

"Are *supposed* to be doing," Akiko broke in.

"Just what does that mean for us?" Vaughn continued. "That we'll never get our careers out of the circular file unless we learn to lie, cheat, and steal with the best of them?"

Akiko shook her head sadly, a small smile crossing her face. "Just how did you *ever* graduate from college, young man?" she asked. "With so little ability to understand what anyone's saying, and such poor self-esteem that you blame yourself for everything . . ."

"C'mon," Vaughn said, crumpling a piece of scrap paper and tossing it in Akiko's direction. "Tell me what you're trying to say, then, without the lawyer-speak, will you?"

Akiko slung her backpack over her shoulder. "Just that in the CIA, everything isn't always what it seems," she said. "Right now, we're on the bottom, and some other people are on the top, right?" she asked. "Except I'm not one hundred percent convinced that that's how it really is."

Vaughn just looked at her. "And this is entirely just a hunch on your part?" he asked. He didn't know whether to feel relieved that he wasn't getting fired or annoyed that Akiko hadn't heard any real gossip.

"Yup," Akiko said. "But remember, I can tell when Blanche is about to hit her brother or when Eugene is going to fall down the stairs from three rooms away. Mothers," she said, tapping her forehead, "have pretty good hunches."

"Fine," Vaughn said. "Tell me whether I'm going to go for pepperoni or lo mein when I finally get home tonight."

* * *

The next morning, Vaughn arrived to find a thick expanding file on his desk chair, courtesy of the archives of the Historical Intelligence Collection. As if she'd wanted to grind it into their faces how poorly they understood the directorate of operations, Betty had recently ordered summaries of a series of successful operations in the Middle East, South America, and Russia. Going through the raw field data in the reports, Vaughn had started to notice code names that kept repeating. After doing his own research on the Web and in various directories and finding nothing, he'd ordered some related files from the Historical Intelligence Collection to see if anything that wasn't classified would come up—or if he'd get the typical reams of reports so heavily black-lined that they still said nothing.

Lifting the heavy file onto his desk, Vaughn noticed a piece of what looked like scrap paper stuck to the bottom. He took it off and was about throw it into the trash when a familiar name caught his eye.

10/4/76 3:11 A.M. VOX to IRIS re: STRIKEOUT

Agent Vaughn rendezvoused with #######
at 1100 hrs and again at 2200 hrs at Loca-
tion ##. DD at 2300 hrs. ####### ##### retrieved
from DD location at appx 2400 hrs. Agent
Harlow made second contact with #######
and ##### successfully completed.
####### ##### payment to Adler & Co. AG
Zürich #######-##########-### for next five
successful transactions pending DO approval.

Although too much of the report was black-lined
for Vaughn to figure out exactly what was going on,
a few things were clear. This was a typical cable from
the field, involving a dead-drop, retrieval, and pay-
ment to an asset at his or her Swiss bank account.
The relevant code names and account numbers had
been deleted, of course, but Vaughn wasn't interested
in them anyway. He was interested in the names of
the agents that had been left untouched.

Agent Vaughn . . . and Agent Harlow.

"Hey, Akiko," he hissed over the cubicle. "Did
any other Agent Harlow work at the CIA in the sev-
enties?"

Akiko's head popped up over the side. "I don't
know. Why?"

"Just find out, will you?" he asked. "I think it's important."

Akiko looked from side to side to see if anyone else was watching. It was lunch hour, and the floor was deserted. "If you're trying to figure out if Betty's ever been married," she said. "I know for a fact she never was."

Vaughn looked up from the scrap. He was mesmerized by the torn piece of paper with its old-fashioned typeface. It was as if he'd just received a letter directly from his father. "Huh?" he said.

"Betty was never married," Akiko said, looking disappointed that Vaughn hadn't asked how she knew. As if she'd measured his level of distraction, she went whole hog. "She told me once, when she was discussing her concerns for my family," Akiko snorted. "Like sticking me in a dull job really makes my husband's life a lot easier."

"Could you find out if there was some other Agent Harlow around anyway?" Vaughn asked. Something he'd just thought kept ricocheting around in his head, and he needed to go home right away and see if his suspicion was correct. He only hoped that he still possessed the documents to prove that what he was starting to suspect was true.

"Sure," Akiko said. "Do you need me to handle

those?" she asked, nodding toward the stack of folders from the intelligence archives.

"Yeah," Vaughn said, sticking the scrap in his pocket and grabbing his coat. "Go ahead and get started. I'll be back in about an hour."

As he walked out of the wide bank of doors at the front of Langley, one idea kept repeating in his head. *It's as if I've just received a letter directly from my father.*

What if the notebook his mother had sent him was exactly that?

As Vaughn reached his car, his thoughts starting racing. It had been ridiculous to think the CIA had sent something to test him or that they routinely tampered with the mail of their recruits, Vaughn now realized. That really was just part of the paranoia the job produced—the wilderness of mirrors. But it wasn't ridiculous for his mother to suspect that they might check his mail or his phone—and to take the precaution of acting accordingly when she sent him something that dated from his father's days at the CIA.

Whatever I told her about Geneva, she definitely knew I was joining the CIA when they came to interview her for my security clearance, Vaughn thought. *But for some reason, she didn't want to let me—or them—know that she knew. But why?*

The answer was obvious. *For my own protection,* Vaughn thought. *After all, she never knew the exact circumstances of my father's death, did she? But when she knew that I must be going into the CIA too, she wanted to let me know whatever* he *knew.*

But was the notebook really a record of his father's days at the CIA? And even if it was, how was he ever going to crack the code to read it?

As he spun his car out of the Langley parking lot, Vaughn didn't know the answers. He also didn't know why Agent Harlow hadn't told him she'd worked with his father.

But he was going to find out.

8

VAUGHN STRODE BACK INTO Langley with the proof he was looking for in his jacket pocket. He needed to show it to Akiko immediately and make sure he wasn't crazy or mistaken.

But as he reached the cubicle area, he sensed something in the air. Akiko was standing up in his cubicle, wildly shuffling through the folders in his overflowing boxes. She turned to meet him, her eyes large and serious.

"Vaughn. Thank heaven you're back," she said.

Vaughn suddenly felt panicked. What was going on? Was it possible that Betty had realized he was looking into his relationship with his father—already?

"What's going on?" he asked, desperately hoping that he hadn't put Akiko in a bad position yet again. Then he felt a sudden surge of anger. Ever since he'd met Betty Harlow, it seemed he'd been second-guessing himself, trying to live up to some ideal image no one would provide or explain. The whole time he'd been a candidate, and the whole time he'd been a trainee, he'd been judging himself harshly, and it seemed that those around him had only been too happy to do the same. But now he was sick of it. He'd done nothing but put his heart and soul into his work at the CIA, and if that wasn't good enough for them, he'd damn well take himself to some organization that appreciated what he had to offer.

I've also got a right *to know more about my father,* he thought, blood pounding in his ears from the sudden rush of emotions. *This organization took him away from me before I had a chance to get to know him. If they can tell me anything about him now, they owe it to me to let me know.*

By the time Akiko replied, Vaughn had worked himself up into such a furious lather he barely heard her. "Vaughn, Betty's called a meeting with the director, and she wants those reports from yesterday. Did you have a chance to finish them?"

Vaughn took a minute to process Akiko's words. A meeting—about his father? But if so, why would she want the reports? Perhaps to complain that his work was subpar?

"Did you finish them?" Akiko repeated, leaning over his computer to click through his hard drive.

"No, I didn't get a chance to," he said. "Listen, Akiko, I have to talk to you about something."

Akiko turned around and glared. "Vaughn, can't you see I'm trying to get us prepared for the meeting?" she said. Suddenly her face went white. Vaughn turned around. Betty Harlow was standing outside his cubicle, watching them with her usual unreadable expression. *This talent of sneaking up on people must have served her well in the field,* Vaughn thought. *How long has she been standing there?*

What came out of Betty's mouth was exactly what he expected and precisely what he least wanted to hear. "Don't worry about the reports, okay?" Betty said. "Let's just get started."

As they followed Betty down the hallway toward her office, Vaughn felt as if he were headed for the guillotine. Akiko turned and sent him a wordless, questioning, *What did you do?* look. *Don't worry,* he tried to project back. *This doesn't have anything to do with you, and I'm not going to let you take the heat along with me again.*

Betty, he thought, watching her long gray pony-tail swing over her jacket like the end of a hangman's noose, *if you mess with me, you're going to get it back this time—in spades.*

* * *

Betty held the door to her office open until Vaughn and Akiko had entered, then shut it behind them, tossing some folders onto her desk. Vaughn had expected to see the director seated there, but the office was empty. "Please go ahead and take a seat," Betty instructed them, lifting one of her files. She began to leaf through it absentmindedly, squinting at certain sections and perusing its contents as if Vaughn and Akiko weren't even there.

Akiko's face had taken on a stony look, as if she knew what was going to happen and was incredibly displeased about it. *Believe me, Akiko, I will do everything possible to make sure you do not get fired,* Vaughn thought. *Betty might have it in for me because of whatever happened with my father, but she's going to have to understand that whatever is happening here, you have nothing to do with it.*

Betty finally looked up. "I'm sure your first months with the CIA have not been working out exactly as you've expected," she began.

Vaughn had never been fired before, but he was sure that *that* line could be found in most corporate guides to gently releasing those employees who had, for whatever reason, just not worked out.

"I'm hoping that what I say next will be somewhat of a relief, and, in fact, something you've expected for a while," Betty continued.

Vaughn saw that Akiko's lower lip had begun to tremble. He couldn't stand it anymore—this was brutal. He had to do something to stop it and to set this situation right side up again before Betty had finished her speech. "Officer Harlow, I'd like to speak to you in private, if possible," he broke in.

Betty looked up in surprise and put the folder down. "Of course, Vaughn. But I'd like to brief you and Akiko on this mission first, if that's all right."

I'd like to brief you and Akiko on this mission first.

Vaughn and Akiko exchanged tentative looks, which then turned to startled and delighted smiles. *Did you just hear what I just heard?* Akiko's eyes seemed to say. *I heard it, but I'm not sure I believe it,* Vaughn thought back, raising a quizzical eyebrow.

Betty had continued, undeterred. "For various reasons it was necessary that you remain at Langley for a period before we placed you in the field, but there's a breaking situation in Brazil that requires your immediate attention." She pushed two of the folders she'd been carrying forward on her desk and nodded at Akiko and Vaughn to take them. After a moment, they leaned forward and opened the files, and Betty began to speak.

"ProTem is a multinational company run by the three gentlemen you see before you—Raul Suarez, Gadi Muhammed, and Dmitri Ruslanovitch, whom the Agency refers to as Triple Threat. They were roommates at Oxford in the nineties, and they've been trying to cash in on every big business craze since then—technology, bioengineering, you name it."

Akiko and Vaughn exchanged glances. Were they going to be investigating some shady company's finances? Akiko had often told Vaughn that she'd left the justice department precisely to avoid that kind of grueling, how-many-decimal-points-can-you-fit-on-the-head-of-a-pin kind of work.

But Vaughn's fears were precipitate. "ProTem is a different sort of company entirely," Betty went on. "Supposedly, it's working to set up environmentally friendly businesses in emerging Third World communities, and it's the first such company to really take off—they reported net profits totaling over one hundred million dollars in the last quarter alone."

"So what's the problem?" Akiko asked, leafing

through the folder. "And why isn't this an issue for the IRS?"

"Bear with me," Betty smiled. "The problem is that it's all a front. And we've been hard-pressed to come up with the proof we need to move on them."

"A front for what?" Vaughn asked. The minute he'd realized that his worst fears were not actually going to be realized, his heart had begun pounding in an entirely new and different way. *It's finally going to happen,* he thought. *Not only am I not getting fired, I'm actually being sent on my first mission!*

Betty laced her fingers together. "A variety of things, actually. When they first set up ProTem, we suspected they were funneling munitions from the former Soviet Union into various terrorist groups in the Middle East. They scotched that pretty quickly, though—the trail was becoming too easy to follow. Now we think they've moved into a bigger sphere from simply being the middlemen."

"Let me guess," Vaughn said. "They're not just having ten-year-olds crochet a bunch of pot-holders."

Betty smiled again—a genuine smile. "Not exactly," she said, her expression darkening with her thoughts and becoming serious. "We think they've moved into the realm of biological warfare."

"Anthrax?" Akiko asked, sitting up.

"We don't know exactly what kind of biological agents they've developed, or the amounts they've stockpiled so far. Your mission is to determine what's going on at Triple Threat's new facility and destroy it, if need be. We've got an agent already stationed in the field, Steve Rice, whom you'll co-ordinate with to determine the next step."

"So where are we headed?" Vaughn asked, straightening the tie he knew would soon come off for whatever disguise he'd be required to wear. One thing was for sure - it wouldn't be a wrinkled gray suit and black shoes.

Betty stood up. "You're going to São Paolo. And you don't have a minute to waste."

* * *

The hour or so that had passed between the time of their meeting with Betty and the moment when Vaughn and Akiko boarded a military cargo plane headed for Brazil passed mostly in a blur. First, they'd been given their covers. They would be traveling as journalists covering an event at the embassy, a party welcoming Nicole LeRoc, a French pop singer and the fiancée of the prime minister's son. International paparazzi were flocking from all over the globe to photograph the happy couple, and

Vaughn and Akiko, outfitted with cargo vests and thirty-five-millimeter cameras, would pass unnoticed in the mix. Their contact, Steve, was undercover as a journalist working for the Associated Press. He'd have almost unrestricted access to the party and would be there the entire evening, making sure that Raul, Dmitri, and Gadi stayed put for the night. Vaughn and Akiko would head over to Suaraz's sprawling compound, which was about a ten-minute ride from the embassy. There, they would get the photos the CIA needed.

"Now, this looks like a normal camera, right?" Barry, the technical consultant, explained. "And it is—you can use it to take photos. Smile, click, you know the drill."

"Barry, get *on* with it," Elena, his partner, commanded. Vaughn thought the two technical consultants looked like fraternal twins, both with long, dark ponytails, glasses, and the same mushroom-white skin. Maybe the CIA grew techies in the basement instead of recruiting them.

"But flip it over and it's a control system for the *real* camera we've got going here. Okay. Are you ready?"

"Barry, how could they be *ready*?" Elena said, moving in front of him and snatching the second camera. "You haven't explained what this *is*." She turned to Akiko and Vaughn. "This is the UAV we've been developing for the past year. Remember those old model airplanes you could fly around the yard?"

"My daughter has one," Akiko said.

"Well, the technology on this baby is a little more complicated, and we hope it'll stand up to windows and trees better. But basically, you buzz it over the structure, and it's able to send a sound wave that sees through walls. I don't want to get into specifics, but you'll be able to tell how large the structure is and what's inside. It doesn't do color, but we're working on that." Elena looked at Akiko and Vaughn expectantly. "No laugh. Well. Just kidding. But Steve's familiar with the equipment—he should have no problem getting you up to speed."

"You skipped the best part," Barry said, looking over at Elena with a sullen expression.

Elena groaned. "Fine. Barry, do you want to tell them?"

Barry shrugged. "Why? I mean, you're doing such a good job and everything, I wouldn't want to—"

Elena threw up her hands. "Fine. Now, this looks like an ordinary film container, right?"

"Sure," Vaughn said, wondering whether Barry and Elena were actually going to come to blows.

"But it's not," Barry said, coming forward with a triumphant grin and snatching the container from

Elena. She sighed and went back to her gray steel stool, where she spun around disconsolately. "You've seen all those movies where the goons come in and take the film out of your cameras and unwind it in front of your eyes?"

"Barry," said Elena exasperatedly.

"Well, they can do that all they want," he said, his eyes gleaming behind his lenses, "Because the real camera is your film *cases*." He handed Vaughn the device, which looked like an ordinary film black container. "See? Nothing out of the ordinary, right?"

Vaughn inspected the cap and plastic tube. "No. But where's the clicker?"

"Here's the beauty part," Elena said. "You put the cap on and click to get your photos. So if anyone sees anything, you're just loading your camera and putting the film case neatly away."

Vaughn put the cap on the container and heard a faint click. Elena turned on the monitor, where a picture of the room was loading. Vaughn was amazed—even though the container couldn't be more than an inch or two wide, it had taken a wide-angle photo of the room, catching all its elements and inhabitants in clear focus. "Ugh," said Elena. "I gotta do something about this hair."

Vaughn handed the container to Akiko and she

clicked in his direction. Another picture appeared, this one including Vaughn.

"Okay. Got it," Akiko said, turning to Vaughn. "Are you ready?"

Vaughn couldn't wait. "I've never been more ready for anything in my life," he said.

* * *

The C-130, a military cargo plane, took off into the sunset, setting all the assembled duffel bags and steel compartments askew. As soon as the rattling had died down, Vaughn headed over to the bucket seats where Akiko was wisely catching up on some sleep in preparation for the hours they'd be spending in the field.

"Akiko," he whispered, gently nudging her shoulder. "Akiko!"

Akiko woke with a start, then gave Vaughn a look of horror. "Vaughn—what is it? Has something happened?"

Vaughn took a seat next to her. "No. But there's something I've been trying to tell you for a while."

Akiko gave a massive yawn. "Vaughn, only you would need to talk about something personal when we're about to head into a nest of terrorist thugs," she said. "All right, I'm all ears. Tell me."

Vaughn took the tattered notebook and the letter he'd retrieved from his apartment out of his pocket. "Okay, see this? This is a letter my father sent me when I was seven and in hockey camp."

"You went to camp when you were seven?" Akiko asked, taking the envelope with its faded script across the front.

Vaughn smiled. "I didn't really go away—it was just a day camp. But I wanted to be a big kid and get mail at camp so badly, my father sent a letter to me to our house asking how it was going."

Akiko smiled. "That's cute. Did you write him back?"

Vaughn laughed, remembering. "I must have written him about thirty letters that summer," he said. "Even when camp was over, I still wrote him and told him what I was doing every day. Sometimes he'd even take me to the mailbox on our corner to mail the letter."

Akiko raised her eyebrows and handed back the envelope. "Vaughn, that's a beautiful memory, but is this why you woke me up out of a very happy, deep sleep?"

Vaughn opened the notebook and placed the envelope next to it. "Okay. Would you say that this is the same handwriting?"

Akiko looked briefly, then more carefully. "Yes.

You've got the repeating break in the twos—that's odd. And the same downward left stroke through the seven. Your fives are identical, too—this writer does his in two steps, and he rarely connects the final stroke to the first one." She looked up at him. "Vaughn—what does this mean?"

Vaughn looked down at the notebook and the envelope, clenching his fists. "Right around when I got recruited by the CIA, this notebook got mailed to me at an unpublished address. I thought it was from my mother, but now I'm not so sure."

"Did you ask her?" Akiko asked.

Vaughn shook his head. "I got worried—I thought it might be some security test the CIA ran on recruits. Then I got worried it really *was* from my mother and she had sent it because there was something she needed me to know about the CIA." Vaughn kicked the seat in front of him. "If she wanted it to be a secret, I didn't want them to find out about it if they were tapping the phones or anything."

Akiko nodded. "When I first got recruited, David used to make jokes all the time about how they were tapping our phones and how all they'd get were Blanche and Eugene talking to my mother. The security clearance checks they run are pretty intense—I don't think it's out of the question. But since every recruit's convinced they're tapping the phones anyway, it's probably not necessary for the CIA to go ahead and actually *do* it."

Vaughn held the notebook up in front of Akiko. "Does this look like any of the standard codes we run?"

Akiko ran her hand over the notebook. "I'd have to look at it more carefully," she said, turning a few pages. "But what do you think is, anyway? What do you think your father was doing?"

Vaughn looked Akiko full in the face. "I think this is my father's diary from before he got killed at the CIA. But first of all, I don't know how my mother got it, and second of all, I'm worried about why she sent it to me."

"Maybe she thought there was something in it you needed to know," Akiko said.

"Maybe," Vaughn replied. "But what?"

9

TEN HOURS LATER, WHEN the plane finally touched down, both Vaughn and Akiko had been able to catch up on most of their sleep. Vaughn woke refreshed, recharged, and half convinced that all that nonsense about a meeting with Betty, Triple Threat, and setting off on a mission to São Paolo had just been a beautiful dream.

From across the aisle, holding a tin cup of water and a toothbrush, Akiko smiled over at him. "You didn't imagine it," she said. "You're still here!"

Vaughn stood, trying to shake out the pins and

needles in his feet—the accommodations on military planes were practically lethal to a body's circulation. "I hate it how you always know what I'm thinking," he complained. "Next you'll tell me that I'm dying for some pancakes and coffee."

"We'll have to investigate breakfast options in Sao Paolo," Akiko mused.

Those options turned out to be dry rolls and watery coffee from the airport as they sped toward the safe house in a very shaky cab. "This is not exactly what I was hoping for," Vaughn said. "Let's hope there's some more options at the safe house," Akiko said, turning to the driver to let loose a burst of Portuguese that he responded to with vehement gestures.

"We're lost," Akiko said blandly, leaning back to sip her coffee behind sunglasses. "The driver also very nicely told me what he thinks of tabloid reporters."

"Tell him we'll feature him with an alien baby if he doesn't get us there in one piece," Vaughn said, looking with trepidation at the floor of the cab. He could almost swear that he saw the ground through a widening rust hole at his feet, rushing by at close to seventy miles an hour.

About twenty minutes later, they'd reached the safe house without incident. As Akiko paid the driver, he exploded in another burst of Portuguese, peeling off in an angry squeal of tires and noxious exhaust.

"Portuguese is an amazing language for telling people off," Akiko said, pushing her glasses up on her head and smiling. "Untold creative possibilities."

"You've got to let me know some of the juicier ones sometime," Vaughn said with a grin. "Or maybe I'll take a refresher course myself."

"Let's just say this: I wouldn't be surprised if that guy really *did* have an alien baby at home," Akiko laughed as they went up the walk. They were in a neutral, almost suburban district on the out- skirts of the city, with rows and rows of unassuming houses and almost no people in sight.

"I'm thinking this probably isn't one of your more luxurious safe houses," Vaughn groaned, heft- ing his pack firmly up on his shoulders and fum- bling for the keys.

"I hear there's one in Paris with two Jacuzzis and a steam bath," Akiko offered unhelpfully.

"I'll keep that in mind," Vaughn said as he swung the wrought-iron outside door open and pushed his key into the lock of the wood-paneled interior one. "Give me a hand with this, will you?" he asked, thrusting his pack onto Akiko and giving the door an extra shove. "It's stuck or something."

Vaughn fumbled with the knob of the door for a moment, then tested it with his full body weight. He'd just pulled back to give it a full-throttle shoulder-shove when the door was suddenly pulled open from the inside. Vaughn went careening into the dusty hallway, slamming his shoulder straight onto the parquet floor and giving his knee a good whack on a side table for an extra measure.

"Ouch!" he bellowed, staring up at the figure that had just released him into extreme pain. Framed by the sunlight of the doorway, the man was an unreadable silhouette, but as he leaned down to give Vaughn a hand, the light from the window struck his face and his features came into shocking focus.

From ten feet away on the floor, Vaughn could hear Akiko's gasp of surprise. He himself could barely speak.

"You gotta be kidding me," he said, still unable to believe it. *"Nick?"* Nick Pastino grinned and dropped to a squat beside the prostrate Vaughn. "Golden boy," he said heartily, leaning over to slap Vaughn on the shoulder. "You always have to make the big, dramatic entrance, don't you?"

* * *

Moments later, Akiko and Vaughn were sitting on the beige couch in the nondescript living room, and Nick—whose real name was Steve Rice, Vaughn had learned—was puffing away on a cigarette and bringing them up to speed. "So I'm sure you wondering who in the hell I really am, and what I was doing at the Farm with you," he said, a cloud of smoke surrounding his square jaw and five o' clock shadow.

With his easy manner, quick laugh, and dry wit, Steve Rice barely resembled the ludicrous hothead they'd detested almost a year ago, Vaughn realized, still amazed, almost trembling from the brief confrontation. As Steve continued to speak, Vaughn kept seeing his face shift from Nick to Steve and back to awful Nick again.

"We've been looking into Triple Threat for some time," Nick said, tapping his ashes into one of the Coke bottles that seemed to double as ashtrays scattered all around the living room. "When you met me, I was at the Farm on a tip that Triple Threat had squirreled a mole into the facility as a CT."

Akiko shook her head. "So let me just get that straight—you were *not* a trainee, right?" she asked, waving away the cloud of smoke that was coming her way.

Nick looked at the burning ember he was holding aloft, then smiled apologetically. "Sorry about this—it's the job. One thing you learn down here: *Everyone* smokes. And that goes double for journalists."

"I hope that doesn't mean we have to pick it up while we're down here," Akiko said, going into a violent coughing fit.

"Nah," Steve laughed, trying to wave the smoke away from Akiko. "I think for twenty-four hours you're safe. But if I hadn't picked these up," he said, gazing at the withered brown filter held lightly between his yellowed fingers, "I would have been found in a ravine a long time ago."

The smoke didn't bother Vaughn—his mother had smoked two Gauloises every evening until he was around five, when his father had insisted that she stop and she'd switched to chewing gum. He still associated the smell of smoke with his happy childhood, when they had all been together as a family. It was endearing him to Steve, somehow. "So how long have you been looking into Triple Threat?" Vaughn asked him.

"Ever since they started," Steve replied. "Ever since I started at the CIA, actually. About ten years."

Vaughn couldn't believe it. "How old *are* you?"

he asked. He started to feel a little bit better about his and the team's performance in relation to Nick's—*Steve's*. They hadn't been facing off with a newbie, after all—they'd been working against a CIA veteran of nearly a decade.

Steve grinned, taking another drag of his cigarette. "That's classified," he said. "But let's just say I was *reallllly* struggling to whip you all on those five-K runs, all right?" He ground out his cigarette in a plastic lid coated with some unknown moldy substance, frowning. "The wife's going to kill me if I can't give these up after this mission," he said, shaking his head sadly. "Can't have them around the kids, you know."

"You bet!" Akiko said, smiling with a look of surprise and pleasure. Vaughn found himself grinning too. Now he *really* couldn't believe it—not only was jerky Nick Pastino actually charming Steve Rice, he was a married man with children!

"Wonders never cease, huh?" Steve said, reading their expressions while he leaned back to unscrew the cap from one of the few Coke bottles that seemed to have escaped the ashy fate of its partners. He took a long sip, his Adam's apple bobbing up and down. "Oh—hey, I can't offer you guys a drink or something, can I?" he asked. "You must be totally tired out from the flight."

Vaughn and Akiko glanced around the room, which looked a lot like the living rooms of frat houses Vaughn remembered from college, filled with empty cans and bottles, dirty plates, forks, and socks, with a thin layer of dust all over everything. He didn't even want to think what the kitchen might look like.

This new Nick might be a great guy, Vaughn thought, *but cleanliness is definitely* not *one of his virtues.*

Steve read Vaughn's mind. "Sorry about this place, bro," he said, finishing off the bottle, tossing it on the floor, and letting out a loud burp. "The cleaning lady who usually does the place has the mumps, and we don't like to change personnel too often, you know?" A mischievous sparkle came into his eyes. "Hey, Akiko, maybe you could get on it while you're down here, huh?" he asked.

Both Akiko and Vaughn were about to rise up in mutual indignation when they suddenly got it and looked at each other, grinning sheepishly. "How long did it take you to perfect the personality of Nick Pastino, anyway?" Akiko asked.

Steve pounded his chest and let out another huge burp. "No time at all, really. I just looked at every disgusting, sexist, aggressive, moronic male trait I saw around me and combined them in one convenient package," he said proudly. "The burping was all me, though—you can ask my wife."

"I'll take your word for it," Akiko replied.

Steve laughed. "My wife says I'm still slipping into Nick a little too often for her comfort," he said.

"I can imagine," Akiko said dryly.

Vaughn was fascinated by what Steve and Akiko were revealing about their marriages. Evidently, they'd been able to work their private lives into their public personas so that the double life an agent led didn't make their relationships suffer. If he could crack the code in his father's diary, maybe he would find out that his parents had shared something similar. *I shouldn't throw everything away with Nora,* Vaughn suddenly thought, picturing her long hair and cowboy boots and dazzling smile. *Maybe it would be possible for me to make it work if I just told her enough about this crazy job.*

But he still had some questions for Steve. "I guess I understand why you went undercover as Nick," he said, feeling a shudder of dislike even as the name passed his lips, "but what was going on with all the physical stuff? Why'd you tackle me that time, and what was going on with your behavior toward everyone else?" Despite the fact that he now knew that the man he was angry with didn't even exist, Vaughn still felt a hot surge of rage at the thought of the sweep-kick that had left him on his back and the public fight that had left him vulnerable to more self-doubt than he'd ever experienced in his life.

"Sorry about that, buddy," Steve said, giving him an honestly apologetic look. "But to let you in on that, I'm going to have to explain some things about Betty first."

"*Someone* should," Akiko said testily. Even though Vaughn was sure that they had both done a lot of rejiggering in their opinions about Betty on the flight to São Paolo, he knew that he still hadn't quite forgiven her for all the hell she'd put him through, and from her burning expression, it was clear that Akiko hadn't, either.

"Well, you know it's typical for the instructors to put the CTs through all sorts of psychological testing and crap," Steve began. Vaughn and Akiko nodded. "Well, not all the testing is out in the open, exactly."

"So what do you mean?" Vaughn asked. "Are you saying that you were a *test* for us?"

Steve took a crumpled pack of cigarettes from his pocket, looked at them longingly, then put them away with a sigh. "Let's just say that Betty likes to get the most out of John Q. Public's tax dollars," he said. "Officially, I was there to investigate the mole. Extra-officially, I was there to see how you all would react to a world-class jerk in your midst."

"You were our psychological obstacle course," Vaughn said, relief beginning to creep back into his bones. Was it possible he hadn't screwed up royally after all?

"And how did we do?" Akiko asked, leaning back against the back of the couch with a glance toward Vaughn.

Steve took the pack out again, considering, then suddenly threw it across the room, where it landed behind a bookcase. He immediately removed another pack from his jeans pocket and stroked it wishfully. "You did well. You know, physical bombs aren't the only kind you ever have to defuse," he said, looking at Vaughn and Akiko meaningfully. "A lot of the bombs you'll meet up with in the field are of the human variety."

"And did we defuse you?" Vaughn asked, unsure. It had seemed like they were getting to Nick at the time, but he'd left the Farm so quickly after their plan was put into action, it wasn't clear.

"Like I said, you did well," Steve said, standing up and yawning. "You stuck together well as a team, and, on your own, you were basically pretty unaffected by my maneuvers, whatever you were made to think about your performance." He leaned down and yawned again, then smiled. "Betty was *especially* impressed with how *you* two reacted to pressure," he said. "Not that you ever heard it from me."

Vaughn couldn't believe it. "So those assessments were doctored?"

Steve grinned. "Just enough to piss you off," he said. "But you guys didn't let it get you down—you came out swinging, which is what Betty was looking for."

Akiko frowned. "That seems like a pretty messed-up way to deal with your employees," she said. "Making them jump through psychological hoops just to see if they have what it takes to stand up in the field."

Steve nodded. "It's a little controversial at the Agency, too," he said. "Again, you didn't hear it from me. But Betty's had a lot of experience with hotshots who flame out once they get into the real deal. I can't go into detail, but let's just say there were some pretty spectacular breakdowns."

"So Betty makes all the best CTs go through total hell before she lets them get to work?" Akiko asked. "That's unbelievable."

Steve spread his hands in a *What, me worry?* gesture. "Let's just put it this way," he said. "*You* only had to be her assistants. She practically had me working in the Langley cafeteria."

* * *

By the time they'd assembled outside the embassy that night, Vaughn had been filled in on their time at the Farm enough that his ego had expanded back to what he considered its original, healthy balloon. *Hopefully not into the dangerous region that leads to those breakdowns,* he'd thought, checking one last time that the UAV and camera/film cases were firmly strapped into what looked like his paparazzi gear.

"So the physical stuff was just to get on our nerves too?" he'd asked in one of the last of a series of pointed questions to Steve about that difficult period.

Steve had grinned again. "Well, actually, I was kind of just feeling you out," he said, smiling more widely at the look of shock on Vaughn's face. "Not literally, of course. But we couldn't find anything in any of your rooms or files that pointed to who the mole was. I was trying to get a grip on who might be wearing some kind of extra equipment."

"Literally," Akiko mused.

"But our fight *was* totally staged. Betty thought a blowup might be the best way for me to publicly leave the group without you missing me," Steve smiled. "Not that you were going to miss me much, whatever I did."

"So I *didn't* go crazy and beat you up!" Vaughn said, his heart pounding. He hadn't done anything wrong!

"Tomato juice, my man," Steve said, pulling open his collar dismissively to point to where he'd presumably planted the blood packet. "I'm sure you must have wondered how you'd KO'd me when *I* was the one landing all the punches."

"Yes!" Vaughn said, laughing with relief. "I thought I'd really lost it."

"Well, I was trying to make you lose it," Steve said. "But you were just so doggoned patient and correct in disarming all of my provocations."

Akiko leaned over and slapped Vaughn on the shoulder. "I *told* you something weird was going on," she crowed triumphantly.

"Believe me, I'll never doubt your mother's intuition again," Vaughn replied, chuckling.

Steve's face darkened. "I still never figured out who tampered with the tanks that day," he said. "I got called down here too quickly to get to the bottom of it, and since Triple Threat was pulling up stakes in Azerbaijan, we had to get here pronto and figure out just what was going on."

Vaughn slapped his knee in amazement. "So *that's* why you attacked Don for his tank," he said. "You were just trying to get some air?"

"That's right," Steve said. "But since I'd investigated the mole thing and couldn't find anything, it seemed like a good excuse to get a dishonorable dismissal at the same time." He flicked away the ashes from the cigarette he'd finally allowed himself. "I must have given old Don a pretty good scare, though," he said.

"So you didn't find the mole," Akiko said.

"No," Steve said. "We now think that Triple Threat was just blowing some smoke around to pull us off the trail." He waved at his own cloud of smoke to illustrate and smile. "They've gotten a ton of disinformation out there since they've realized we might be on to them. It seems like a lot of the intercepts we've made might be completely false."

"And we're here to investigate whether this one has any truth," Vaughn observed.

"That's right," Steve said, grinding out his cigarette. "And if the world is lucky today, the most dangerous thing at Raul Suarez's compound is the pool in his backyard."

*   *   *

The Suarez compound was only a ten-minute ride from the embassy, and Akiko and Vaughn were prepared to tell any authorities that questioned them that they had simply gotten lost on their way to the LeRoc gala. They entered the compound without incident, though, simply flipping over a small stone wall about a mile behind the house Steve had assessed days earlier and declared alarm-free.

"Cher, we're in," Akiko informed Steve through the wireless, invisible mikes Barry and Elena had fastened like crowns over their back molars. Vaughn began to assemble the UAV and set up the laptop and foldable satellite dish to transmit the images to Langley.

With his Associated Press credentials, Steve was one of the few reporters allowed into the festivities. "Copy that," he replied, the sounds of hubbub and laughter clearly audible in the background. "Hold your position. Repeat: Whitney and Mariah, hold position until I get a visual on our three musketeers."

"Do you think he'll bring us back a magnum of

champagne?" Vaughn asked Akiko, clicking on the laptop to bring up the transmittal bar. The blue bar quickly filled from 1% to 99%, then finally 100%.

"If you get what you came for," Steve replied, laughing—Vaughn had neglected to turn off his mike's Send feature.

"Link established," Vaughn said, knowing he must be blushing even in the dark. "Repeat: Cher, we've got a link."

"All right, I've got a visual," Steve said. "And boy, does she look good enough to eat!"

"Hey, married man?" Akiko replied, setting up the UAV. "Do you think we could put Nick away for the evening and concentrate on our jobs?"

"Sorry," Steve's voice crackled through. "Le-Roc's a little distracting. Okay, I've got our boys at nine o'clock, and we definitely have nothing to worry about. They look like they're polishing off all the champagne in the place, though, Vaughn— sorry."

"All right, let's move," Vaughn said. Clicking off transmission momentarily, Vaughn ran the laptop's control test of the UAV and nodded at Akiko. Wordlessly, she flipped open her camera, and the foot-long plane rose up in the air like a helium balloon.

"Watch the wind," Vaughn cautioned, noticing the leaves rustling angrily in the trees. "I don't want this thing slamming into Nicole LeRoc's face when she's out smoking on the embassy's balcony."

"Got it," Akiko said. She had already guided the glider toward the region over the house, and the laptop had begun to spit out a stream of digits, sending them directly over to Langley, where they'd be converted into 3-D images and sent back via satellite.

"Whitney and Mariah?" Steve's voice came through the headset, sounding far more animated and tense than before. "We've got movement from our three musketeers."

Akiko's voice was equally tense. "Delay them, Cher," she said. "I've got about five minutes of fly-over time left before we'll have what we need."

"We've got definite movement," Steve's voice came back. "Repeat: definite movement from our boys. Finish your stuff and get out of there—I'm going to try to hold them up."

Vaughn could picture Steve running after them in the crowd, holding up his reporter's pad and asking them a few questions about ProTem. Would it be enough to hold them off? And how could they possibly know about the UAV so soon—was their alarm system so sophisticated it could detect it? Even though Vaughn was no expert, he was pretty sure that was impossible.

There had to still be a mole in the CIA—someone with enough access to information to let Triple Threat know what was going on almost as it happened. But the only people Vaughn knew with access to that information were the three of them, Betty, and the director of operations.

Who's telling Triple Threat what's going on here? Vaughn silently wondered.

Ticking down the seconds frantically, Vaughn and Akiko finished the flyover and retrieved the UAV. Packing it up as quickly as they could, they leaped over the fence and returned to the road just as a black Mercedes with tinted windows roared up the drive. Slamming themselves into a small dip by the side of the road, Akiko and Vaughn just missed getting caught in the glare of the vehicle's headlights.

"Back to the safe house," Vaughn whispered to Akiko. "Double-time."

When the vehicle had made its way to a safe distance up the drive, they leaped out of the gully and back onto the road, where they hailed another cab—thankfully, this one not as decrepit as the first—and made their way past the crush of vehicles around the embassy.

"Lots of big party tonight," the driver commented, trying out some clearly rudimentary English as they inched their way by. "Lots of pretty people."

"Yes, lots," Akiko agreed. Vaughn kept trying to get Steve back on the line, but he was getting nothing but air.

"Cher?" he whispered, keeping his lips almost clamped together so the driver wouldn't observe anything out of the ordinary. "Cher, do you copy?"

There was nothing.

Back at the safe house, Vaughn and Akiko dropped their gear and immediately set up the satellite station again. The phone rang. "Thank God," Vaughn said, striding over to pick it up. Perhaps Steve had gotten caught in a crush of reporters whose network of global transmissions might well be blocking his own. Whatever it was, Vaughn would be glad to know that the man was all right— he'd started to like Steve as much as he'd disliked Nick.

But when he picked up the phone, the voice on the other end of the line was Betty's. "We've lost satellite contact with Cher," she said immediately. "Mariah? Whitney? Do you copy?"

Grimly, Vaughn answered in the affirmative. "Wait for further instructions," Betty said, then hung up the phone. Vaughn didn't need it spelled out to him. It was clear what had happened. Even though they'd gotten the photos, the mission was a complete failure.

Triple Threat had gotten Steve Rice.

10

VAUGHN HIT THE DESK in frustration. "We can't just leave him there!" he yelled at the circle of faces.

Betty had immediately called them back to Langley after it was clear what had happened, and Vaughn had spent almost three hours trying to convince her and the director that they needed to send in an extraction team after Steve. Although they'd lost audio feed with him back at the embassy the night before, Barry and Elena had finally been able to pick up a very, very faint GPS signal still being emitted by the mike embedded in his tooth. The only problem was that the signal they were picking up was coming from Azerbaijan.

"So they took him back to the original location of their operations," Vaughn said. "We know Suarez has a private jet Triple Threat uses all the time—it makes perfect sense."

"Or they just flew the whole tooth to Azerbaijan," another tech suggested, looking innocently at the horrified faces around him. "What?" he asked, putting up his hands. "You know it's a possibility. They've been trying to throw us off their tails the entire time we've been looking into them. It would make perfect sense."

"First of all, the chances that someone would remove a tooth and take it to Azerbaijan is ridiculous," Elena said, vibrating with so much anger that Vaughn thought she was going to crumple her Styrofoam cup while it was still filled to the brim with hot coffee. "Not to mention highly unlikely, since the entire apparatus is lodged in a filling and virtually undetectable. Second, Barry and I designed the GPS to feed off of body heat, so unlike the mike, it's entirely thermal. That's why we can still hear it. For your theory to work, you'd have to have a person removing a filling they could never see or sense in the first place, then holding it close enough to their own bodies that it was as hot as the inside of a mouth—which is a lot hotter than the surface of your skin—and therefore still working. I'm sorry, but it doesn't fly."

"So you're saying that the chances are very good that Steve is still alive," Vaughn said.

Elena looked around at the room, then back at Vaughn. "They only pay me about one-third of what I'm really worth at this dump, but I'd stake my entire yearly salary on it, personally," she said, downing her coffee in one large gulp.

"For whatever it's worth, I would too," Barry said, raising his hand tentatively, then, when no one responded, putting it back in his lap.

"What worries me," said Betty, "is the possibility that they know *we* know where Steve is, and they're just waiting for us to come get him. I don't fancy sending a group of my agents into a trap."

"But that's why we've *got* to get him," Akiko said, sounding as if she was growing more frustrated by the minute. "The fact that they bothered to take Steve with them at *all* points to the strong possibility that they already know he's CIA. Once they get whatever intel out of him they're looking for, his life isn't even *worth* what we could bargain for on it, if we move fast enough."

"I agree," the director said, ending the nearly three-hour debate with the first words he'd uttered yet. "I think we need to get an extraction team in, and let's get it in now. We've lost valuable time already."

Betty turned to look at Vaughn and Akiko. "Are you up for going? You'll be coordinating with the people we've already got in Azerbaijan. They're working on some intel we've picked up from wiretaps in the area."

Vaughn didn't hesitate. "Get me on a plane," he said.

Akiko nodded vigorously. "Me too," she said. "We've worked with Steve before, and we know how to use our strengths to complement his."

When I first met this guy, I wanted to kill him, Vaughn thought. *Now I'm about to get on a plane and risk my life to save him.*

* * *

This time, there was no rickety cab providing transportation from the airport to the safe house. They were met at the field by Don, who had grown ruddier and a little thinner since the last time they'd met.

"Long time no see!" Don yelled, waving them over. He reached over to give Akiko an awkward hug, then slapped Vaughn on the back, grinning. "You guys have a good trip?" he asked, leaning over to spit a stream of tobacco. Akiko jumped back, startled. "Oh, sorry," Don said. "Everybody chews here, you know."

"I'm starting to think all that stuff about tobacco being addictive might be true," she said sarcastically, shaking her head at Don as he walked them to the car.

They passed through the hot, dusty streets, avoiding the occasional loose chicken or other car racing past in the other direction. "So, you guys get anything off of your photos on that mission?" Don said. "Boy, we'd sure love to get something so we could move on that crew—they left here just as I came over, I heard."

"No," Vaughn said distractedly. Something seemed strange about Don, but he couldn't put his finger on it—the tan or the weight loss, maybe? "The photos got back to Langley okay, but there was only evidence to show that they were setting up a manufacturing space—nothing to point to there being anything down there for sure."

"The mission got interrupted," Akiko said briefly. "Where are we headed, Don?" she asked.

Don turned around to grin at both of them, and

Vaughn realized what was different—he was wearing glasses. He hadn't worn glasses at the Farm—
no one did. There were too many paramilitary
maneuvers to make it practical. "The safe house, I
toldja," he said. "Why, do you have to go to the
bathroom?"

Something was tickling at the edges of
Vaughn's brain. Something about the glasses. Don
and his glasses.

In their first meeting, Don had claimed to be a
former air force pilot and aeronautical engineer.
But he couldn't have been an air force pilot with
glasses. *The air force only allowed people with
20/20 vision to become pilots.*

It was possible, Vaughn surmised, his thoughts
racing, that Don had only recently gotten the
glasses and that nothing funny was going on. But
Vaughn's funny bone was feeling pretty funny to
him, and as he looked over at Akiko, he saw that
hers was, too.

Using the unspoken communication they'd per-
fected during almost two years of working together,
they acted immediately and in sync. Vaughn
slipped off his belt and pulled Don's head back in a
sudden choke hold, and Akiko drew her weapon
and brandished it near his face.

"Hey!" Don said, his eyes widening and his

grasp on the wheel becoming weaker. "What do you guys think you're doing?" he sputtered, taking one hand off the wheel to pull at the belt. Vaughn released it—slowly.

"Don," Akiko said in a steely voice, her eyes narrowing. "How did you know about our mission in São Paolo?"

Vaughn was only holding the belt tightly enough to restrict Don, not enough to choke him. Still, the impulse to tighten it grew stronger with the conviction that they were right. "*You're* the mole," he hissed in Don's ear, wishing he could take out the anger he was feeling on the slug in front of him.

"Guys, stop being crazy," Don pleaded, trying to gesture with his hands and steer at the same time. "You know they brief us on all the operations over here!"

"Brief you, sure," Akiko said. "Tell you an agent's been taken and why. But the only ones who are briefed on individual missions *are the ones who are going on them,*" she said, biting off the words and pushing the gun closer to his ear.

"It's the first rule of operations, Don," Vaughn agreed, giving the belt a little tug just for his own satisfaction. "It's for your safety and ours—and Steve didn't get away too safely."

"Big coincidence," Akiko said, pushing the gun into his skin.

Don's driving had slowed to a near crawl, and Vaughn released his grip a little. Don let out a rattling breath and hit the gas hard.

"Don't get any funny ideas, Don," Akiko said, keeping an eye on the road. "First you're taking us to Steve, and then we're taking you back to Langley in leg irons."

"C'mon, guys," Don said desperately, sweat beginning to pop out on his skin. "I can cut you in on it! There's enough to go around for everyone, believe me," he said, and began to blubber.

"Sure—that's why someone was waiting for us at the safe house, right?" Vaughn asked, jerking the belt again. "Someone with some nice leg irons for me and Akiko?"

"Or someone to put a bullet in both of our heads," Akiko said.

Don suddenly began to laugh, a wild, crazy, hysterical laugh that scared Vaughn even more than the thought that Steve might have already been shot. "You guys think you're so smart," he began to chatter. "But you're not smart at all."

"Oh, yeah?" Akiko asked. "Pull over and you'll see how smart we are."

Don's laugh became louder. Before Vaughn and

Akiko could stop him, he did a desperate 180-degree turn into an alleyway on the other side of the road. The car came to a screeching halt and rolled forward momentarily into complete darkness. Suddenly, Vaughn was blinded by a rack of bright overhead lights.

Throughout the few seconds of helter-skelter driving, Vaughn had maintained his grip around Don's neck, but now he saw that Akiko had been thrown back against the car door, her pistol lost somewhere in the junk littering the floor of the car. He also saw that they were surrounded by goons—goons who were pointing Uzis straight at Akiko and him.

Vaughn released his grip on Don's neck. The goons gestured for Akiko and Vaughn to open the car doors and get out, then yanked their hands behind their backs and secured them painfully with handcuffs.

Don stepped out of the car, still blubbering and laughing at the same time. "You said to take you to Steve," he said in a childish, high-pitched whine. "And I did! I did! I did!"

A blond giant strode across the room. "Shaddup," he screamed in a Russian accent, slapping Don across the face. "Stupid loud American," he muttered, looking more closely at Vaughn and

Akiko. "Do you stupid Americans have anything to say?" he asked, cracking his knuckles.

"Dmitri Ruslanovitch, I presume," Vaughn said. "Where are the other two musketeers?"

The giant came toward him and drew back his hand. Then everything went black.

*　*　*

When Vaughn came to, he could hear the soft sounds of Akiko's voice mingling with someone else's. In his hazy, just-waking-up state, he first thought it was Nick Pastino. *But that's silly,* he told himself. *Akiko hates Nick—why would she be talking to him?*

As if his head had suddenly been doused in cold water, he came to violently. His head *had* been doused in cold water, he realized blearily, looking up at the stream that was trickling from the pipes over his head. He just thanked heaven that it hadn't been the waste pipe that let fly on him.

"So you've joined us, golden boy, have you," someone called from across the room. Vaughn tried to see who it was, but everything looked blurry and strange. "I can't see you," he called, hoping the voice was Steve and not his imagination.

"That's courtesy of Dmitri Ruslanovich, who

gave you a very nice pair of black eyes. He's been giving me some in the last couple of days, too, but I've had a little more time to heal."

"Steve!" Vaughn cried joyfully. "You're alive!"

"Of course I'm alive," Steve growled. "Thank god for this thing in my tooth—I was praying the whole time that Raul wouldn't knock this one out when he was taking his swings at me. I lost a few, sure—but no molars. Where's the goddamn extraction team when you need them?"

"We're here," Vaughn said. "We had the misfortune to run into Don on our way over, though."

Steve made some clicks with his tongue that Vaughn assumed were supposed to be sympathetic. "*You're* my extraction team?" he said. "No wonder we're all padlocked to pipes in the basement."

"Where *is* this placc, anyway?" Vaughn asked. He could barely remember the car ride—they'd had a grip on Don, and then he'd escaped somehow. He tried to make out the shapes around him, but they were just a mass of blacks and grays, with an odd, squat red square thrown in for good measure.

"This is the factory we should have been looking at the whole time!" Steve spat out. "I thought that operation in São Paolo stank from the beginning, and I was right. They were just trying to throw us off from their real work here. Triple Threat hadn't pulled up stakes here at all—they'd just transferred ownership to your good friend and mine. . . ."

"Don," Vaughn and Akiko chorused.

"Right," Steve said, making a long, dragging sound with his chains like Jacob Marley's ghost. "And if I had half a thought rattling around with these marbles in my head, I'd have figured it out long ago."

"Well, don't feel too bad," Akiko said. "They did have a hundred million dollars' worth of technology to jerk us around with, you know."

Vaughn was starting to feel the pain creep into the wooly, dense area that had previously housed his eyeballs.

"This is a rare event, actually," Steve said. "Having all the boys at the old homestead at the same time—it almost never happens anymore. It seems they found the thought of three agents to kick around at the same time too good to pass up."

"That's all they're going to do?" Vaughn asked. "Kick us around?"

Steve was silent for a moment. "Well, first they're going to kick old Don around and make sure he's not playing both sides, you know? Tipping off the CIA to who Triple Threat has decided to kidnap this or that week. Then they're going to come kick us around and see if they can figure out how much the CIA knows about what they've got going on in this burg, and then—"

"Then they're going to dump our bodies because it's taking too long and pull up stakes here and start again somewhere else," Akiko finished.

Steve sighed. "Yup, m'dear," he said. "That seems like pretty much *it.*"

Vaughn couldn't believe it. He was almost on the verge of a hysterical breakdown, and Akiko and Steve, who both had families, were blasé to the point of being absurd. *Hey, guys, can we do some quick thinking to get out of here?* Vaughn thought, but couldn't bring himself to say it. *I don't want to spend my last days being beaten to death in a basement, and I'm sure you don't either.*

Maybe they weren't saying anything because they'd thought through all the options—and there weren't any.

Vaughn felt a surge of nausea, whether from his wounds or from the harsh turn his thoughts had taken, he couldn't tell. "And the CIA won't be able to prosecute them," he muttered, breathing raggedly, "because they won't have any proof to pin anything on them when they come up for air."

"Well, no—not unless you consider those pictures I got at the embassy of three men dousing themselves with champagne proof of a crime, which I almost do," Steve said. "But then, we didn't have time to get those pictures of their factory in Brazil, did we, so we'll never know. The CIA might as well strike it off their list—those guys'll never use it again." He sighed, a deep, rattling sigh that seemed to encompass all the sorrow in the world. "That crew knows it's hot." Vaughn couldn't tell if he was sad because of their situation or because the CIA had lost the right to stake out the house in São Paolo.

Suddenly Vaughn's right leg, the one that was chained to the pipe, became hot so fast that at first he thought it was a sympathetic reaction to Steve's uttering the word.

Vaughn jerked his leg so violently that he pulled the thin pipe partly away from the wall. A gush of searing water streamed out from the jagged edge, splashing right onto Vaughn's lower half. As much as it hurt, Vaughn clenched his lips together and tried to not to scream, slowly edging the chain down around the edge of pipe so that his lower body was freed.

"Vaughn, what's happening?" Akiko shouted across at him, but Vaughn couldn't talk for the pain.

"Shhh," Steve said. "Don't wake the beasts."

The gush slowed to a trickle. Almost losing consciousness again from the pain, Vaughn slowly maneuvered around on his stomach so that the chains holding his arms were on the very edge of the broken pipe. Gritting his teeth, he pulled.

"Aw!" he screamed, unable to hold it back. The pipe had cut such deep gashes into both of his arms that for a moment, he didn't realize he was freed. He lay in a heap on the floor, unable to speak.

There was a flurry of footsteps on the stairs, then someone threw the door open. "What's going on down there?" a voice asked in a British accent. Another voice, this one murmuring in Spanish, chimed in, and then the door slammed again.

Vaughn didn't need a translator. The voice had said: "Let's finish up with Don. We've got to get this going right now."

It was clear what was happening—Triple Threat was on the move, and it was time to finish the job. If he didn't do something right now, they would all be dead within a few minutes. Vaughn heaved himself upward with a groan. "I'm out," he croaked, trying to keep the gray shapes in the room from spinning out into nowhere.

"Vaughn, we only have a minute," Steve said urgently. "Get yourself out of here and come back for us—it's the only way."

"Vaughn, go!" Akiko whispered. "Get out while you can."

Vaughn shook his head blearily. He forced himself to focus on the red square in the corner—it might be some kind of worktable, he thought. He only hoped it contained something that could break the fragile pipes holding Steve and Akiko. *Thank God they never replaced the plumbing,* he thought.

Vaughn staggered over to the table, feeling as if he had the worst hangover in the history of time. A series of shapes swam up to meet him, and he realized he'd smacked his head on the table and fallen. "Vaughn, on your left," Akiko whispered, realizing what Vaughn was looking for. "Grab the pipe on your left!"

Vaughn lifted it and staggered backward again, having overcompensated mightily for the weight of the object, which he'd assumed was pinned down. "Got it," he said, hoping the blood flowing down his arms wouldn't make the pipe too slippery to hold.

He fumbled his way in the direction he heard Akiko's voice coming from, but she urged him back. "Get Steve first!" she said. "Then he can get me out—you're not going to last that much longer, Vaughn!"

Steve's voice came from across the room. "I usually like to let a lady go first," he said. "But I'm going to have to agree with Akiko on this one, friend."

Vaughn pushed himself over to direction of Steve's voice, feeling as if he were dragging three bodies behind him. He saw a square of light and came to a stop. "Okay, you're right in front of me now," Steve said calmly. Vaughn looked down. He thought he could see a large beige shape, like a seashell, rising in the center of his vision.

"Strike for nine o'clock, my boy," Steve said. "And strike hard."

Above their heads, there came the sound of running footsteps, then a shot. It was now or never. Vaughn gathered all the strength he had left. He stopped feeling the blood pouring down his arms and the searing pain in his legs. As if he were playing a carnival game, trying to bring a hammer down and ring the bell at the top of the pole, he slammed his pole with all his might.

There was a satisfying crack. "Now that," Vaughn heard Steve say, as if from a great distance, "is what I call teamwork."

Vaughn fell to the ground to the sound of rattling chains and hissing and the sudden noxious smell of gas. Through a dim haze, he felt Steve grab the pipe from his arms, run across the floor to Akiko, and begin to strike at the pipe she was lashed to. "Got it," he heard Steve yell triumphantly, and in the next moment he felt Akiko's arms lifting him to his feet.

"Vaughn, we're getting out of here," she said desperately. "I don't care if I have to drag you, but you have got to try to stand up at least, okay?"

He heard the cellar door fly open and the sound of footsteps on the stairs. Behind him, someone was breaking glass, and there was the rush of wind and light striking his face. He felt arms lifting him, then dragging him away on the rough ground. There were more shouts from the basement, coming closer.

He heard a click, and soft whirr, like a lighter being struck.

"My lady," Steve murmured to Akiko. "You are about to be so glad that I had that smoking habit."

VAUGHN AND AKIKO SLOWLY walked away from the crowd of mourners dispersing from the dark gray headstone at the top of the hill.

It had been a brief graveside service, with only Steve's immediate family and a few other officials from the CIA in attendance, Betty among them. Steve's children turned out to be red-headed twin girls and an older son, a tall, somber boy with Steve's dark hair. The expression on his face brought back memories of the *other* CIA funeral Vaughn had attended.

No one could have predicted what had

happened after Steve had tossed the lighter into the basement with its hissing pipe of rapidly dispersing gas. Steve had thrown himself on top of Akiko and Vaughn to shield them, and he'd done that job—his last—successfully. But his own body hadn't been able to withstand the force from the large chunk of the outer wall that had collapsed in the explosion and fallen directly onto the three of them.

Steve, Vaughn had thought over and over again during the three weeks he was in the hospital recovering. *Steve, Steve, Steve, Steve, Steve.*

He'd awakened to find Akiko sitting at his bedside. This time, there was no confusion. He saw the bandages on his arms and legs, he knew what he did for a living, and he knew exactly where he was.

"Steve's dead," he said simply.

Akiko looked back at him. A nurse rushed to his bedside and began to check his vitals. "Yes," she replied. "Now can you tell me your name?"

Nearly a month had passed since then, and his physical wounds had healed. The mission had been a success—the bodies of Triple Threat and Don Hewitt had been recovered from the rubble, and ProTem was no more. But as he walked from Steve's grave, his heart hollow, Vaughn knew he would never entirely recover emotionally from the loss of the man who had saved his life.

He and Akiko walked back to the car in complete silence. He knew that it would be a while before he was ready to speak again. As he went to the passenger's side to open the car door for her, he saw that tears were spilling down her face, and her shoulders were shaking with sobs.

"Hey," Vaughn said, putting his hand on her shoulder briefly, then helping her into the car, leaning past her and around to put the seat belt over her small shoulders. "Hey, shhh," he said, clipping the metal clasp into place.

"They were so *young,*" Akiko choked, covering her face with her hands.

For a minute, Vaughn had no idea who she was talking about. But as he walked around to the driver's side of the car, got in, and put his key into the ignition, he finally realized who the "they" was: Steve's children.

"Akiko, they'll be all right," Vaughn said, letting the keys fall into his lap for a second and putting his arm around her shoulders. "Losing my father was the hardest thing I ever had to get through. But all my life, I've believed that he didn't die in vain." Vaughn took a deep breath, trying to keep back the tears that were creeping into his own eyes. "I'm following in his footsteps now, and I know that working for the CIA is also a way of honoring how he died." He squeezed Akiko's shoulder. "What Steve died for is important, Akiko—he saved our lives, and his work will allow a lot of other families all over the world to stay safe."

Akiko caught a rattling sob midway up her throat. "But I want *my* family to stay safe, Vaughn," she protested. "And I never realized just how much I did until now."

Vaughn rolled down the window to let the unseasonably warm air waft into the car. He could still hear the voices of other mourners walking back to their cars and the rumbling sound of their engines turning over.

Akiko had calmed herself down and was wiping her eyes with a tissue. "I know the work we do is valuable, Vaughn," she said, her chest still heaving with choked sobs. "It's only today that I've realized that I'm not willing to give up my life for it."

Vaughn couldn't believe what he was hearing. "But you must have thought about this before!" he said, trying to keep the emotion out of his voice so that he didn't upset her further. Akiko couldn't pull out now, he thought—not when they'd just completed their first mission. It wasn't right, and he wasn't going to let it happen. She was grieving for

Steve and his family—and so was everyone else. But he had to help her get over it—and get her back to work.

Akiko smiled sadly at Vaughn. "Of course I've thought about it," she said. "And my feelings haven't changed—I'm as willing to give my life for my country as I was before. But what I'm realizing," she said, wiping new tears from her eyes, "is that I'm not willing to leave my children without their mother."

Vaughn couldn't help what came, unbidden, to the front of his thoughts. *Did my father ever think about the fact that he might die in the line of duty?* he asked himself, realizing that he'd been pushing the thought down ever since he'd known for sure that Steve was dead. *Did he ever decide that he was willing to let me go?*

He shook off the train of thought. "Akiko," he said. "You're just upset because of the funeral, and—"

"I'm not *just* anything, Vaughn," Akiko said, her voice sounding small and defeated. "This has been coming on for a while—I just haven't felt sure enough to say anything. Today was the last straw in a long line of straws."

Vaughn was quiet, realizing that Akiko was serious. "Is there anything I could say that would make you change your mind, Akiko?" he asked. "I mean, you're my best friend. I don't think I would have made it through the Farm without you. And I certainly can't imagine working at the Agency without you."

Akiko pulled Vaughn into a tight hug, starting to cry all over again. Then, just as quickly, she released him and blew her nose noisily into a second tissue she'd pulled from her pocket. "Uch! You're going to be the end of me, Vaughn," she said. "Look at me—bawling all over you like a baby."

"You can bawl on my shoulder anytime," Vaughn said honestly.

Akiko waived her tissue dismissively in his direction, reminding him of how she'd shaken her keys at him in the parking lot of the Holiday Inn on the first night they'd met. "Vaughn, the next time I want to bawl on your shoulder," she said, "is the day you finally marry that girlfriend of yours."

* * *

The following Monday, Vaughn was scheduled to begin work again back at Langley. He decided to ask Betty for some time off to go and visit his mother, whom he hadn't seen in the last two years. The funeral had reawakened powerful feelings, and he was almost desperate to get home, just to check that his one living parent was safe and sound.

He was also thinking very strongly about paying a visit to Nora.

On the way to Betty's office, he looked into Akiko's cubicle with dismay. She'd already cleared out her desk and removed all the photographs and notes she'd kept pinned against the spongy, fabric-covered plastic walls. On his desk chair was an envelope in her handwriting with his name written across the front.

"Oh, Akiko," he muttered, stuffing the envelope in his pocket to read later, in private. "Did you have to leave before we could even have a last lunch?"

He walked over to Betty's half-open door. "Do you have a second?" he asked, knocking lightly on the wood and poking his head in.

"Of course, Vaughn," Betty said, standing briefly until he took a seat. She sat and looked him over with concern.

"I'm thinking I'd like to take some time off," he said, bracing himself for a negative response.

"Of course," Betty agreed immediately. "We even recommend it in these situations. Of course, we also have counselors available for you to speak to, if you'd like to look into that."

Oh, sure, Vaughn thought sarcastically. *So you can think I'm some weakling who can't handle this kind of stuff.*

But what she said next was the last thing he'd ever expected to hear from her. "I saw a counselor after your father died," she said quietly, staring straight into his eyes and nodding. "Yes. And it was more of a help to me than anyone will ever know."

Vaughn's mind was reeling. He couldn't believe what Betty had just said.

"You're going to talk about my father?" he asked. "Now—after everything that's happened?"

Betty nodded slowly, like she'd come to some decision. "Vaughn, I know your time here has been difficult, and that there have been times that you've doubted my methods with you." She laughed. "Believe me, when I was working with Steve, there were times that I doubted them myself."

Vaughn still couldn't believe what he was hearing. The great Betty Harlow had suffered from self-doubt?

"One thing you should never doubt," she said, "is that for your entire time with the CIA, I've been behind you one hundred percent."

Vaughn exploded, unable to keep his emotions in any longer. "But you've been keeping me from finding out about my father's death," he railed. "You worked with my father—I've seen the files. And you've never mentioned it to me at all— you've never let me find out what *happened* to him."

Betty's lips settled into a thin line. Vaughn was worried he'd angered her until he realized she was trying to keep herself from crying.

"Vaughn, I loved your father," she said care fully. "He was my partner and my good friend. When he died, I didn't think I'd ever get over it."

"Sure," he said bitterly. "You loved him so much, you've been trying to get me kicked out of the CIA since the minute I walked through the door."

Betty nodded, as if she'd expected him to say that. "I don't try to claim that it hasn't been diffi- cult for me to see you working here after what happened," she said. "You look so much like your father, and—" She smiled sadly. "Let's just say that sometimes it's like having a ghost walking around."

"Right," Vaughn said. "A ghost who isn't half the agent his father was."

Now Betty's face became genuinely angry. "Don't you *ever* think that, Vaughn," she said. "It's true that your father was an excellent agent—one of the best the CIA ever had. But that doesn't mean he didn't have his doubts. I've never thought it was fair how all his files have been sealed to your family."

A creeping suspicion began to form in Vaughn's mind. "It was you," he whispered, only half daring to believe it. "It was you who sent the notebook to my mother!"

Betty remained expressionless, neither nodding nor shaking her head to give away anything. "Your father always kept a diary," she said. "In all this time after his death, we've never been able to locate it."

"*You* had it, and you sent it to my mother," Vaughn said. "And she thought it might be something important, so she sent it on to me with that weird note—because she wasn't sure how to handle the situation, knowing what she knew."

Again, Betty didn't give anything away. "I'm afraid I don't know what you're talking about, Vaughn," she said, all business again. "Like I said, the diary was never located." She looked straight at him again. "I can assure you that no one in this Agency has ever read it."

She kept it away from the brass all those years, Vaughn thought. *For my family—and for me?*

Vaughn stood up, his voice breaking. "Thank

you," he said, reaching out to shake Betty Harlow's hand.

Betty took his hand and gave it a firm shake. She didn't say "You're welcome."

But Vaughn could feel her thinking it.

* * *

The wisteria outside his mother's home had grown nearly high enough to reach his chest. The last time he'd been there, it had barely reached his ankles.

"Maman!" he cried like a five-year-old as his mother came into view at the top of the weathered driftwood stairs, then came flying down the steps to meet him. He'd slipped back into French as if he'd been speaking it every day for the past two years. "You look fabulous!"

Amélie Vaughn had always been a very pretty woman, but in the years following Vaughn's father's death, her features had fallen into a mask of melancholy, and her straight black hair had gone ashy gray. Now the hair was pure white, and his mother's vivid blue eyes stood out from her healthy, tanned face as she looked at him with joy. *"Michel—* finally! You've come home to visit! I thought we were never going to see you again," she scolded, grabbing him by the arm and, with her measly hundred-pound frame, attempting to haul Vaughn and his bags physically up the stairs.

"I'm coming, I'm coming," he laughed, taking his bags back from her and hastening up the stairs in her wake.

Vaughn had always loved coming back to his mother's house, always filled to the brim with her paintings, good wine, and the wonderful smell of her cooking. But now, at the top of the stairs, his mother hesitated, then put her finger against Vaughn's mouth. "Someone is here," she said clearly in English. "Someone that I would very much like you to meet."

For a moment, Vaughn was terrified that his mother, always eager to get him married off, had somehow convinced Nora to make the trip across the country in an effort to seal the deal. But he dismissed the thought as ridiculous. Even his matchmaking mother would never go that far.

"It's not those cousins you were always talking about, is it?" Vaughn joked as they crossed the threshold, immediately regretting his words as he observed the small, bearded man standing at the center of the room. With his olive complexion, the man looked very European indeed. Who could it be—Vaughn's long-lost uncle, perhaps?

"This," his mother said, as if announcing an act at a comedy club, "is Jonas Van Dyck. Jonas," she said, turning toward the odd man and gesturing to Vaughn, "this is my son, Michael."

"I've been hearing about you for a long time," Jonas said, walking over to take both of Vaughn's hands in his own. Vaughn clasped them back, still confused.

"I haven't really heard anything about you," he said, turning to his mother with a questioning glance—he hoped he hadn't insulted the man, whoever he was. But if he'd only ever met him as a young boy, he certainly couldn't be expected to remember him now. "Um—who are you, exactly?" he asked awkwardly.

Jonas laughed a great big booming laugh, and his mother's delicate laughter rippled above it. "My boy," he said, clapping Vaughn heartily on the back. "I believe the term your generation has brought into common use would be *boyfriend*. That is, I am your mother's boyfriend."

Vaughn's mother nodded, drawing Jonas closer and smiling at Vaughn. "I wanted to tell you before," she said plaintively. "But I just couldn't over the phone, and it didn't seem right to do it by e-mail."

"We're planning on getting married next summer," Jonas declared, puffing out his chest like a twenty-one-year-old who'd just been given his first drink at the bar. "And all I need from you to make her say yes is your blessing."

Vaughn's mother looked at him, her eyes shining. "Well, *chéri*?" she asked, slipping one hand in his and the other in Jonas's. "Do we have it?"

* * *

Resting in his room before dinner, listening contentedly to the laughing and clinking of glasses and the music of Billie Holliday drifting up from the kitchen, Vaughn thought back over the past week. First, there'd been Steve's funeral. Then Akiko had quit on him. And as if that hadn't been enough, his mother had revealed that, even at sixty, she was still capable of starting all over again, with a new life and a new marriage.

Would Vaughn ever be able to start on his first?

Akiko! Vaughn suddenly realized that after his tumultuous meeting with Betty, he'd forgotten entirely about her letter. He hadn't left it dangling on some hanger at home, had he? He scrambled over

191 — THE PURSUIT

to his favorite jacket and felt the smooth, long rectangle. It was still safely tucked in his pocket. Withdrawing the envelope, he breathed a sigh of relief.

He opened the letter and began to read.

Dear Vaughn,

Sadly for you, this is not going to be the good-bye note that I know you've been looking forward to all weekend (ha-ha). After I met with Betty, she absolutely refused to let me leave the Agency— not just because I'm a great officer, you understand, but mostly because she seems convinced I'm going to sell all my secrets to the highest bidder. We worked out an agreement— I'm going to be the new director of the CIA's Center for Families, which will coordinate all the activities for spouses and children. This works out great for us: no more day care for Blanche and Eugene (hooray!). As you can see, I've already moved my stuff into my new office, which is far swankier than the old one (though I'm sure you'll be out of this cubicle soon enough), and you can reach me at extension 6754. Give me a call—if you're nice, maybe I'll take you to lunch on my new expense account.

Love,
Akiko

Vaughn couldn't believe it—Akiko hadn't left the Agency at all. The whole time he'd been mourning the pain of her loss, she'd simply been setting up her new office in another division—one with far better perks, from the sound of it. Maybe he should think of getting into the family racket himself.

"Michel?" he heard his mother call from downstairs. *"Depêche-toi! Nous sommes prêtes!"*

Get into the family racket . . . with Nora?

As he went downstairs, he saw the glowing candles on the birthday cake before he even realized it was for him. "We wanted to celebrate your birthday with you," his mother said, taking his hand and leading him to his seat at the head of the table, where she placed a little cone hat on his head, "Because we have missed it these last few years. Jonas is responsible for the hats," she added quickly.

Vaughn looked at the candles on the cake. . . . They were adding up very quickly. Was his mother trying to send him a hidden message? Was she trying to tell him that time passed quickly—and that he should grab whatever wonderful things came his way as tightly as she had her entire life?

And as tightly as Steve and his father had?

"Life takes enough away from you," he remembered her answering when he'd asked her, after his father died, why they had to move to California. "I've always wanted to live there, and now we shall, while we still have the chance."

As if she'd read his mind, his mother leaned over to stroke his hair, then began to speak quietly while Jonas fiddled with his camera in the corner. "Your father and I were very happy," she said. "Now I have found Jonas, and my life would be complete if only I knew that you had found someone who could make you happy too."

He swallowed, suddenly feeling ridiculous in his child's hat. He snatched it off his head, hoping Jonas hadn't already captured the moment. "I may have, *Maman*," he said. "But I don't know if she's even interested anymore."

Now his mother smiled fully, her Gallic sense of romance lending a dip to her lower lip. "Well, you will not ever know if you do not go and ask her, will you?" she asked.

Vaughn leaned over and blew out the candles just as Jonas, who had finally figured out his camera, momentarily blinded him with its flash. He figured that the blindness, for now, was symbolic of his mental state.

"I wished that you two would have the happiest marriage I know," Vaughn said, leaning over to plant a kiss on his mother's cheek. "But can we start with the *pot-au-feu*? I'm so hungry I could eat this whole cake myself."

* * *

The trip to New York to see Nora was easier to arrange than Vaughn had thought it would be. He kept expecting crises to get in the way: Nora's e-mail would have changed, she wouldn't answer her phone, she would refuse to see him even if she *did* answer the phone. But when he reached her at home on his first try, she sounded thrilled to hear his voice, arranging to meet with him that Saturday afternoon at Augie's, a small jazz bar on the Upper West Side near where she lived.

Vaughn arrived early, with a huge bouquet of peonies—her favorite—in his hand. Even as he walked up Broadway, his heart was racing—he wouldn't be surprised if she didn't show up after all.

Well, what do you expect, Vaughn? he asked himself. *You dump her and tell her you're leaving the country, then you're AWOL for practically two years, and suddenly you show up to ask her if she wants to consider getting back together . . . and maybe even-*

tually marry you? You've got to admit, for a guy who usually dots his i's and crosses his t's with a ruler, you're not coming off as a very stable prospect right now.

Yeah, but she stayed out of touch too, his other side argued back. *You didn't dump her—you both knew you had to figure out your careers before you could embark on anything serious. Now she's set, you're set, and there's nothing holding you back from each other.*

That's if she's still interested in you at all, his other side replied. *But I guess that's what you came here to find out.*

You better believe it, Vaughn told himself, shutting off the voices in his head and pushing open the door to Augie's. It took his eyes a moment to adjust to the dark, and then he saw Nora, seated at a table in a far corner by the window.

She had not changed so much with the years as she had deepened. Her hair was a warmer chestnut, her eyes even darker. Even her voice sounded throaty as she rose to greet him. "Hello, Vaughn," she said, the dimples standing out in her cheeks as she smiled. Vaughn caught the familiar scent of her perfume over the smell of old cigarettes and whiskey from the bar.

He was reaching across the table to hand her

the bunch of peonies he'd gotten her when he suddenly stopped and blushed. Nora, he saw, had changed in another way too—a *big* way.

She was pregnant.

Nora laughed and took the flowers, leaning across to plant a slightly awkward kiss on each cheek—the one "Frenchified" custom she'd never allowed when they were going out. "These are beautiful," she said, smiling at Vaughn's expression, which he was sure still radiated pure shock. "I'm not as far along as I look, honest—I'm only five months. It's just that I've gotten really fat!"

"You don't look fat," Vaughn said seriously. "You look beautiful."

Nora blushed again and laughed. "When you called, I didn't know whether to tell you on the phone or not," she said. "But then I figured, it's one of those things that's easier to tell a person *in* person." Vaughn suddenly noticed the flash of the ring on her left hand—a delicate gold band encircled with diamonds.

"How long?" he asked, not trusting his voice to get out the words.

Nora smiled and laughed again. "It's just been a year. This is a little surprise," she said, patting the mound beneath her coat. "But it's a surprise that makes us very happy."

Vaughn didn't think he could take another surprise, personally—but at least he was learning to roll with the punches.

"I'm very happy for you," he said, not knowing yet whether he meant it.

Nora reached across the table and took his hand, squeezing it in her earnestness. "Vaughn, we had our time, and it was great," she said. "But honestly, after you left me that day in New York, I really believed I would never see you again." Her face became serious. "And for the past couple of years, that's pretty much been true."

Vaughn had known all along that things might not work out, but he hadn't been prepared for the sadness he was feeling now. He'd really lost his chance, hadn't he?

If you die in the field, there'll be no wife at your funeral, he thought.

"Nora, I understand," he said, trying to sound upbeat even though he was getting glummer by the second. "Things were a lot different then, and you were right not to wait for me." He gestured to the flowers. "Even if I did come—finally."

Nora nodded. "Vaughn, I won't lie. I was in love with you, and getting over you was one of the hardest things I've ever had to do," she said, emphasizing the last words. "But at the same time, there was always something unspoken between us—something you could never talk about." Vaughn began to protest, and she raised her hand to stop him. "I don't know what it was, and I don't want to know now," she said, tears coming to her eyes, then finally spilling over her long lashes onto her cheeks. Her voice grew husky. "I'm just very glad to see that, whatever it was, you're all right."

Vaughn placed his hands over hers. "I feel the same way about you," he said simply, trying to accept the situation, since it didn't look like it was going to change anytime soon. "Now tell me all about this guy you got married to."

*   *   *

Whipping down the New Jersey turnpike on his way back to Washington, Vaughn felt his sadness lifting. His thoughts about Nora, he was starting to realize, hadn't been so much about *her* as about the fact that all around him, people were falling in love, working through their marriages, and being together. And although it hurt to think that he'd never know what could have happened between them, he knew deep down that he hadn't been in love with Nora—just with the thought of ending how lonely he truly was.

He'd felt under so much pressure to make a choice—any choice. All around him, people were making decisions—Akiko, Betty, his teammates at the Farm, even his mother. Somehow, he'd thought that if he got a family as quickly as he could, his life would just fall into place around him.

But that wasn't true. Not only because Nora already had started her own family, but because life just didn't work out that way. It wasn't something you ordered off the menu at Burger King, and it wasn't something you could find in other people's lives.

It's not even something I could find in my father's diary, he thought, thinking of the notebook that had fallen behind in a fire that had happened thousands of miles away. *Maybe it's better that I'll never know his private thoughts—at least not before I know myself a little bit better. And meanwhile, I've got my friends, my next mission, and a Whopper at the next rest area I pass,* Vaughn thought, feeling better already. *I'm just going to take it slow.*

Maybe for now, he'd start by getting a dog.